Dear Reader,

Thanks for taking time out of your hectic life to pick up and enjoy a Silhouette Desire novel. We have six outstanding reads for you this month, beginning with the latest in our continuity series, THE ELLIOTTS. Anna DePalo's *Cause for Scandal* will thrill you with a story of a quiet twin who takes on her identical sister's persona and falls for a dynamic hero. Look for her sister to turn the tables next month.

The fabulous Kathie DeNosky wraps up her ILLEGITIMATE HEIRS trilogy with the not-to-be-missed *Betrothed for the Baby*—a compelling engagement-of-convenience story. We welcome back Mary Lynn Baxter to Silhouette Desire with *Totally Texan*, a sensual story with a Lone Star hero to drool over. WHAT HAPPENS IN VEGAS...is perhaps better left there unless you're the heroine of Katherine Garbera's *Her High-Stakes Affair*—she's about to make the biggest romantic wager of all.

Also this month are two stories of complex relationships. Cathleen Galitz's *A Splendid Obsession* delves into the romance between an ex-model with a tormented past and the hero who finds her all the inspiration he needs. And Nalini Singh's *Secrets in the Marriage Bed* finds a couple on the brink of separation with a reason to fight for their marriage thanks to a surprise pregnancy.

Here's hoping this month's selection of Silhouette Desire novels bring you all the enjoyment you crave.

Happy reading!

Melissa Jeglinski

Melissa Jeglinski
Senior Editor
Silhouette Desire

Please address questions and book requests to:
Silhouette Reader Service
U.S.: 3010 Walden Ave., P.O. Box 1325, Buffalo, NY 14269
Canadian: P.O. Box 609, Fort Erie, Ont. L2A 5X3

CATHLEEN GALITZ

A Splendid Obsession

Published by Silhouette Books
America's Publisher of Contemporary Romance

SILHOUETTE BOOKS

ISBN 0-373-76715-3

A SPLENDID OBSESSION

Books by Cathleen Galitz

Silhouette Desire

The Cowboy Takes a Bride #1271
Wyoming Cinderella #1373
Her Boss's Baby #1396
Tall, Dark...and Framed? #1433
Warrior in Her Bed #1506
Pretending with the Playboy #1569
Cowboy Crescendo #1591
Only Skin Deep #1655
A Splendid Obsession #1715

Silhouette Romance

The Cowboy Who Broke the Mold #1257
100% Pure Cowboy #1279
Wyoming Born & Bred #1381

CATHLEEN GALITZ,

a Wyoming native, teaches English to students in grades six to twelve in a rural school that houses kindergartners and seniors in the same building. She feels blessed to have married a man who is both supportive and patient. When she's not busy writing, teaching or chauffeuring her sons to and from various activities, she can most likely be found indulging in her favorite pastime—reading.

For Casey—who inspires me every day with his courage

One

She was going to get fired.

It was the last thing Kayanne could afford at the moment. Financially or emotionally. She could think of nothing more unfair after working so hard to pull herself out of the gutter and back up on her own two feet than proving to be a failure her very first day on the job.

Unless, of course, it was endangering another person's life....

Where could that crazy old lady have wandered off to?

Kayanne scoured the perimeter of the nursing-home grounds one more time and tried to calm herself.

Still no sign of Rose.

Maybe she had just gone for a little unauthorized walk. Kayanne couldn't blame anyone for wanting to escape the bland horror that was the Evening Star Retirement Manor. She just didn't want it happening on *her* shift. Freshly back in town after a ten-year hiatus, she'd felt compelled to return to help her mother recover from a heart attack.

And to make a fresh start for herself.

Had she not so desperately needed any job to advance that goal—even this dead-end one for which she had neither the training nor, apparently, the aptitude—Kayanne would have laughed at the thought of being terminated.

That particular word sent another wave of panic crashing over her. A minimum-wage paycheck wasn't the only thing at stake here. An eighty-year-old woman was lost and at the mercy of fate.

Kayanne's imagination kicked into overdrive. Was Rose ambling into the path of oncoming traffic this very minute? Suffering heatstroke beneath the relentless summer sun? Or hitching a ride out of town with some sicko? If Mrs. Johansson was suffering from dementia, the possibilities were endless.

Kayanne's gut twisted into a complicated knot.

The stress of the runway was nothing compared to being responsible for another human being. Her first concern was, of course, for Rose. Her second was to keep her position—and her tenuous pride—intact without anyone else being the wiser. After all, she'd only managed to land this lousy job in the first place because the person who'd hired her was desperate to find any warm body to fill the late-afternoon/evening shift. And because he had no idea she was the town pariah. It didn't hurt any that J. R. Lemire usually let his hormones do his thinking for him. He'd been so preoccupied with her outward attributes during the interview that he'd scarcely taken the time to look over a résumé that would be far more impressive at a New York fashion house than a retirement home in Podunk, Wyoming.

Tossing a precautionary look over her shoulder, Kayanne bolted across the street and began searching the adjoining neighborhood. Yard by yard.

Half a block later, she was on the verge of hysteria when a high-pitched giggle caught her attention. The charming scene unfolding on the veranda of some stranger's home stopped Kayanne in her tracks.

And left her trembling with relief.

Were it not for the residual adrenaline playing havoc with her nerves, she might have collapsed into a boneless pile right there on the pavement. She couldn't believe that she had worked herself into such a state over a flipping *tea party!*

Suddenly in no mood for exchanging social pleasantries, she threw open the front gate and marched up a neatly groomed sidewalk with the same determination that Sherman had advanced his army to the ocean. Stopping at the bottom of the steps, she employed a voice that had on occasion intimidated some of the best photographers in the business.

"Excuse me, but just what do you think you're doing?"

Ignoring the fire flashing in her caretaker's eyes, Rose smiled sweetly and proceeded to offer up the obvious. "I'm sharing a glass of iced tea with Mr. Evans. Would you care to join us, dear?"

"No," Kayanne snapped, too frustrated to toss in so much as a perfunctory thank you for the offer.

It boggled her mind that Rose had been so close all this time. And was apparently in no mood to be rushed along. The old lady dismissed Kayanne's petulance with a wave of one hand. With the other, she held out her glass for a refill.

The look of pleasure on her weathered face touched a heart considered incorrigible by many claiming to know Kayanne. She stared into a pair of twinkling blue eyes set in a face lined by eight decades of life and caught a glimpse of a young, wild Rose. Unnerved by the image, Kayanne turned her ire on a more deserving target: her runaway's unwitting partner in crime.

The man looked to be in his early thirties. Slim but not slight, with an amiable, masculine face that stopped short of being pretty, he sat on a cushioned wicker chair, making it impossible for Kayanne to judge his height. Positioned behind a laptop computer, he gave the impression of being completely comfortable in his lightly tanned skin.

He stirred in Kayanne a sense of barely restrained fury.

"Actually, I was directing the question to your boyfriend, Ernest Hemingway."

She gestured dismissively at stacks of books piled about the porch and bit her tongue to keep from asking what kind of drivel he was in the process of writing.

The taunt only evoked a grin from him. That he appeared pleased by the comparison drawn to the hard-drinking author made Kayanne frown. That quick smile of his might well disarm someone less cynical, but she had always been more inclined to humor a bad boy sporting tattoos and an attitude than a scholar who might take the time to indulge a confused elderly woman who meandered into his yard.

"All apologies to Hemingway aside, I was just in the middle of writing the great American novel when Mrs. Johansson's unexpected visit distracted me," their impromptu host volunteered in a voice that needed no liquor to make it sound throaty and deep. It wrapped around Kayanne's nerves like a designer silk scarf.

A self-effacing smile indicated that Rose's Mr. Evans didn't take himself nearly as seriously as his words might imply. Blushing to the roots of her silver-blue hair, Rose lived up to her colorful name as she gurgled with pleasure.

"It's been a long time since any man found me a distraction."

Kayanne rolled her eyes. This guy's antiquated charm might work magic on the geriatric set, but it grated on her already frayed nerves.

"Are you sure you wouldn't like a drink?" he asked her. "I'd be happy to fix you something stronger than iced tea if that makes any difference."

Kayanne bristled.

"Why should it?" She wanted to know.

Was it possible that her reputation preceded her to

such an unlikely spot? Or did she have a scarlet *A* pinned to her chest labeling her an alcoholic? One visible to everyone but her.

"Maybe because you seem so frazzled that steam's coming out of your ears," he explained.

An open smile remained affixed to his face in spite of Kayanne's loud harrumph.

"You really are welcome to sit down and relax," he added, rising and offering her his chair.

Kayanne was sorely tempted. Rose was safe and disinclined to leave, the sun was sweltering, and Kayanne felt as rung out as a rag doll. There were certainly worse things than to unwind in the presence of someone so gracious. And good-looking.

Spying an unopened bottle of whiskey perched on the porch railing a respectable distance away from a pitcher of iced tea beading in the afternoon sun, Kayanne reminded herself that she wasn't the best judge of character when it came to men. Reigning in her edginess, she did her best to don a more professional manner. It wasn't easy considering how the receding surge of adrenaline left her feeling as contentious as a boxer.

"I'm working," she said tersely. As if that had ever stopped her from having a drink before.

"Me, too," their host said, flashing her a wicked grin before picking up his own glass and taking a long, satisfying swig.

Kayanne caught the faintest whiff of alcohol. She swallowed hard. When, if ever, would temptation loosen its stranglehold on her? She stuck a hand deep into the pocket of her standard-issue smock to connect with the touchstone that kept her grounded day by day.

And moment by moment.

Her six-month sobriety token was more precious to her than diamonds. It was a physical reminder of how far she had come. And how far she had left to go.

Humbled by her ignominious descent and working on her recovery, she cautioned herself to be on the alert for the kind of behaviors that had caused her to stumble in the first place. She had no business entertaining any thoughts whatsoever about the opposite sex when her sobriety, not to mention her job, was on such shaky ground. Certain that she simply needed to apply the same focus and drive that had launched her career as a successful model to the task at hand, Kayanne set about thwarting any troublemaker who dared to interfere with her attempt to act responsibly.

"I guess unannounced visitors saunter into your front yard wearing their pajamas every day, Mr. Evans," she said, trying not to sound shrill. "Did it ever occur to you that it might be a good idea to call the nursing home next door and report a missing person to the staff there?"

"Call me Dave," he suggested, offering her his hand by way of a belated introduction. "And, no, actually it didn't. Since I just recently moved in, I don't know one neighbor from another, which I assumed Mrs. Johansson to be."

Rose pursed her lips. "I am your neighbor, and I'm not missing. I'm exactly where I want to be."

Duly chastised, Kayanne succumbed to courtesy by

accepting the man's outstretched hand. Just under six feet tall, she seldom had the pleasure of looking people in the eyes, let alone of having to look *up* to meet such a rough and hungry gaze. Or of feeling such an alarming jolt of sexual energy from the exchange of a simple handshake. Telling herself that the absolute last thing she needed to screw up her progress was a sexual interest, she withdrew her hand and anchored it firmly to one hip.

"You can call me Kayanne."

"Like hot pepper?" he asked without any apparent malice.

"Pronounced the same as the spice but spelled with a *K*."

She supposed that the fact that Dave was unfamiliar with her name accounted for his initial lack of animosity. One of the few models prominent enough to warrant first-name recognition among New York agencies, Kayanne mentally repeated Andy Warhol's quote about fame generally lasting all of fifteen minutes. Hers had lasted somewhat longer, but the cost had almost been her life.

Dave's smile failed to hide his primal response to her, but his dark eyes seemed somehow gentler than those of most men who perused her from head to toe without bothering to hide their appreciation of her as a sex object. Other women given to tender fantasies might well fall into a pair of eyes like those and lose themselves in daydreams involving home-cooked meals, adorable children and fabulous sex.

Not Kayanne, who refused to be deterred from her

mission by anything so banal as a potential amorous interest. For someone who associated sex with hitting rock bottom, there was no such thing as a little harmless flirtation. No matter how intrigued her hormones might be, she couldn't afford to focus on anything beyond returning her client to the "Home" without drawing undue attention. As fascinating as this blond, all-American novelist may be, Kayanne wasn't about to be fired for fraternizing with the same fellow who'd nearly caused her a heart attack.

Glancing at her watch, she attempted to bribe Rose into leaving. "If we don't hurry, you'll be late for the movie showing in the rec room. I believe it's *Titanic*."

"I already know how it ends," the older woman said dryly.

Kayanne didn't appreciate Dave's booming laugh. Not only did it serve to encourage Rose, it also reached right inside Kayanne and reverberated in every cell in her body. She resented this stranger for reminding her that she was a woman with carnal needs that hadn't been satisfied for quite some time. Her muscles contracted around a tug of arousal, and she met the interest flickering in his eyes with steely resolve.

It would be nice if, for just once, a man would look past her appearance and try focusing on what she felt inside. Her temper flared to match the color of hair that once graced the covers of some of the trendiest magazines on supermarket shelves.

"Do you think there's a word in your thesaurus that might describe the peculiar relationship you have with a woman so much older than you? And maybe another one to help me get Rambling Rose here back to her room before an all-points bulletin is issued and I lose the job of my dreams?"

To Dave's credit, he only blinked twice before regaining his composure. Leaning his weight on the back of the chair that he'd offered her earlier, he said, "I believe the first word is called *friendship*. Maybe it's not one you're familiar with."

"Barely," Kayanne admitted.

Truthfully, she could think of few people who would risk an alliance with the town's most infamous heartbreaker. So far as she knew, friendship was just a weak substitute that unattractive women used in lieu of romance. And she had yet to meet a man who had so much as a clue what the word meant.

Loneliness coiled through the empty space in her chest.

"The second word that you're looking for," Dave clarified, following up on her line of questioning, "would be *please*."

It was a word that had never come easily to Kayanne. She tested it on her tongue and found it bitter. And tough to chew.

While not exactly looking to claim the title of Miss Congeniality, Kayanne did her best to curb her famous temper. She already had a long list of people to whom she needed to make amends as part of her recovery and didn't need to add yet another name to it.

"Please…" It slipped through clenched lips.

Dave's biceps relaxed as he released his grip on the

chair and rewarded her efforts by turning his pearly whites full force on Rose.

"What d'ya say you ladies drop by again some other day when your visit is sanctioned by the proper authorities so that none of us get into any trouble?"

Rose shot Kayanne a killing glance as she reached across the table to pat Dave's hand affectionately.

"All right, but you should stock up on gingersnaps. They're my favorite. Just in case I decide to stop by again. Say tomorrow. Around the same time."

After a deliberate pause, she added pointedly, "By myself."

"I'll look forward to it," Dave assured her. "But you be sure to bring Kayanne along too. Being new in town, I can use all the friends I can get. I've just signed on at the community college to teach English starting this fall, and I don't know more than a half a dozen people around here."

Ah, that explains it.... Kayanne thought to herself.

After a week of running into nothing but hostility from people who would just as soon kick her while she was down as offer her a hand up, she knew there had to be a reason why this man wasn't taking potshots at her dwindling fame and minimum-wage position.

Or propositioning her...

Kayanne didn't want to delay their departure by refusing Dave's invitation outright and causing Rose to dig in her heels again. As much as she'd love to beat the afternoon heat with a glass of tea and strike up a friendly conversation with someone who couldn't judge her by her past, duty and a pressing need to pay the bills called.

Tomorrow wouldn't be any different in that respect. Unless, of course, she could convince her supervisor to bend the rules, which was highly unlikely. J.R. struck her as the rule-conscious sort who would come to a complete stop at a burned-out red light in a deserted ghost town. At midnight.

"Until we meet again then," Rose said, holding out an arthritic hand to Dave.

Kayanne noticed how gently he took it in his own, being careful not to squeeze too hard. She almost choked when he lifted it to his lips and placed a kiss upon its leathery surface. She was tempted to ask him to kiss another part of *her* anatomy as they took their leave but didn't want to risk upsetting her genteel client with such a vulgar suggestion.

"Would you like any help in getting Rose home?" Dave asked.

"I can handle things from here by myself," Kayanne told him curtly.

The thought of anyone thinking otherwise was intolerable.

"But thank you for offering," she added as an afterthought. "And for everything else."

Such as being so sweet to Rose and so understanding of her own plight. For making her feel pretty instead of dirty for a change. And mostly for just playing along and making a difficult situation more tolerable.

"I mean it about stopping back by again sometime," Dave said. "Don't worry about interrupting my writing. The truth is that I'd be eternally grateful for the diversion."

Having been considered a *diversion* more than once in the past, Kayanne just smiled and put him off as politely as possible. "We'll see."

The likelihood of their paths ever crossing again was slight. Still, she appreciated the invitation more than he would ever know. She couldn't remember a time when a man had made her feel so welcome without expecting something in return.

"Let me see you two ladies to the gate," Dave said, coming around from behind his chair to help Rose up and make sure she didn't fall down the steps.

Delighted with the simple courtesy, she took his arm and gushed all the way to the sidewalk. It was easy to see why Rose was so enamored. In fact, they barely stepped off out of hearing distance before the older woman proved there is no age at which one is safely exempt from the green-eyed monster.

"Why don't you just mind your own business?" she hissed, yanking her elbow out of Kayanne's helping hand.

While she wasn't exactly expecting overwhelming gratitude for her efforts in locating Mrs. Johansson and returning her safely to her room, Kayanne didn't think she'd be attacked for it either. So much for harboring any fantasies about Rose becoming the kindly grandmother she'd never had.

"What are you talking about?"

"If you must know, I'm in love with Professor Evans," she said coyly. "So consider yourself warned, girlie—keep your hands off of him!"

Kayanne tried not to laugh. Rose's crush was sweet,

in a pathetic sort of way, and she saw no reason to point out the obvious difference in their ages. Any more than she needed anyone to call attention to the difference between Dave Evans's and her own background, education and standing in the community.

"Don't worry," she assured her aged companion. "He's not my type."

Rose looked surprised.

"Why the hell not?" she demanded, shattering any remaining stereotypes Kayanne might have had about doddering old ladies. "He's good-looking, smart and damned polite considering how rude you were back there."

Kayanne hoped swearing with impunity was a right one earned with age. At least that would be one thing to look forward to in the future. Why she felt the need to explain herself to a geriatric fugitive was beyond her, but she saw no need to gloss over the truth either.

"I generally go for the rebel type. Fixer-uppers, my mother likes to call them. Personally, I just feel that there's less chance of hurt feelings when the time comes to go our separate ways if both of us are irreparably flawed."

Rose shook her gray head in dismay. "What about your feelings, sweet pea? And don't try and tell me you don't have any."

"My feelings are off-limits."

Rose stopped shuffling her feet.

"Not if you want to get back to the Manor anytime soon they're not."

Kayanne forced herself to take a deep, calming breath. She could scarcely explain to herself let alone to Rose that Dave Evans appeared to be a real gentleman and, as such, was the exact opposite of the kind of man she used to date—before realizing that her sobriety hinged on remaining single.

"Let's just say he scares me."

It wasn't an easy admission for a woman who worked so very hard to appear fearless at all times.

"Or maybe it's just the stifling stability he represents that scares me," she clarified, sorting her feelings out loud.

A stickler for honesty, Kayanne hoped she wasn't lying to herself. For while that statement had rung true in the past, lately dreams of domesticity crept into her thoughts at the oddest times. She assumed it had more to do with her self-imposed celibacy and a desire to carve out a more normal life for herself than the ticking of her biological clock.

"No need to be afraid of a good man," Rose informed her with an unladylike snort. "Unless, of course, he's mine."

Kayanne bit her lip to keep from grinning. As a recovering alcoholic and a has-been model with a reputation as long as Sheridan's Main Street, she stood as much of a chance of hooking up with the handsome would-be Pulitzer prize winner as Rose herself did. Now that the crisis of the moment was behind her, Kayanne took a minute to consider Rose's perspective as they began their slow journey across the street. She had to admit that Dave wasn't hard to look at. And the fact that his charm extended across generations and beyond the bounds of barroom pickup lines said something about his character as well.

He was exactly the sort of man her mother was attempting to pray into the life of an unruly daughter whose homecoming was as much an act of penance for past sins as it was a matter of necessity. Kayanne shuddered at the thought of being attracted to a man her mother actually approved of: stable, sober and undeniably *nice*. One could almost attach the smell of sugar cookies and wholesome goodness to him.

She imagined Professor Evans's classes would soon be overflowing with eager women far more interested in their instructor than anything he might assign them to read in the textbook. With his good looks and easygoing personality, she doubted he'd be lonely long.

Kayanne directed Rose to the back door of the retirement center, hoping to slip her in without attracting undue attention. She didn't have the heart to set the old lady straight regarding matters of propriety. What was the harm in harboring a little romantic fantasy at her age? Just because Kayanne had decided to shelve her romantic dreams didn't mean everybody else had to.

It was too bad Dave Evans was the sort of man who could make a woman regret her decision to take herself off the market.

Permanently.

Two

Dave Evans stopped typing only when it grew too dark to see the keyboard. As the sun dipped behind the Big Horn Mountains and bid him good evening, he stretched out his lean frame, put both hands behind his head and let out a satisfied sigh. He didn't know what to make of the redheaded Amazon who had strode into his yard earlier in the day, but he was grateful to her nonetheless. After weeks of wrestling with writer's block, he'd finally produced something other than tortured prose destined to fill the garbage can.

He didn't dare call this intruder by her real name. Even if their paths never crossed again, Kayanne was far too unusual a name to slip unobtrusively between the covers of a book. The woman who'd trespassed onto his property and into his novel had the same unnerving effect upon his usually aloof hero as she had upon him. Just the memory of those catlike eyes, lithe body and sassy attitude ignited a fire deep in his belly. Although no stranger to physical attraction, Dave couldn't remember ever being broadsided by such overt sensuality as hers before.

Since Kayanne's handshake alone transmitted enough voltage to electrocute a mortal man and she was already threatening to burn up the pages of his previously stalled novel, he could only imagine what she could do in real life between the sheets of his bed….

He reprimanded himself for allowing his thoughts to travel down that shameless avenue. Was this woman so intriguing simply because she was a complete enigma or just because he was feeling alone as a newcomer to the community?

From her unusual name to the defiance that had defined her grasp, Kayanne was unlike anyone else he'd ever encountered. He was fascinated by the challenge flashing in a pair of eyes the color of jade.

Jaded eyes.

Dave suspected those eyes had seen a good deal more of the world than any of the characters he'd invented with their complicated, contrived pasts. Hell, there was more vibrancy in a simple toss of Kayanne's unruly mane than in any of the words he'd so painstakingly fashioned for the cool, blond heroine of his imagination who, as of yet, had failed to dominate either his hero or his novel. His writing was seamless enough in structure to earn him a master's degree, but lately it felt as separated from the nitty-gritty of reality as the ivory towers of academia that defined both his literary style and his life.

That wasn't to say that he hadn't experienced any success as a writer. Reviews of his first novel, *Bitter Fruits*, had heralded him as the next William Faulkner. Unfortunately, he'd never been particularly fond of Faulkner. Nor had the fact that the book had won some literary awards translated into a huge advance for his next novel. Commercial success and literary success were not always one and the same. That reality lay as heavy on his chest as the impending deadline that was kicking his butt. Lately he hadn't been able to produce much of anything except writer's angst, and that didn't translate well to the page.

Dave worried that his parents were right about it being time to give up on his dream of being a full-time writer and academic. John and Eula Evans couldn't understand why their only son would choose to spend his life knocking his brains out over a keyboard in the wilds of Wyoming when he could just as easily take over the family business from the comfort of their Birmingham estate.

Frankly he couldn't understand it himself.

All he knew was that there was a monster inside him that had to be fed a certain number of words every day or it would eat him instead. He was hoping that the obscurity of this remote mountain town would allow him to prove himself on his own terms—and to break through the writer's block that had him so stymied. Simply introducing Kayanne as a minor character took his story in a fresh, new direction and breathed life into words that, up until now, had felt as dry as dust blowing across the vast Wyoming prairie. Dave dubbed his new character Spice, hoping no one would draw the connection between fact and fiction.

At the moment, he was more concerned about not letting this headstrong character take over his whole book. In the span of a couple of pages she was already making moves to push his delicate heroine all the way back to her Tara-like roots. After all the time he'd taken to develop Jasmine as a woman of substance, he wasn't about to let her go so easily into the night—even if the outspoken Spice was of the opinion that she was little more than a simpering fool. Spice might not be the nicest character he'd worked with, but the woman knew her own mind.

And took great delight in playing with his.

Later that night when Dave crawled between the sheets of his bed, he was startled by the fact that it was not his blue-eyed blond creation that played havoc behind his closed eyelids, but rather a long-legged, green-eyed beastess who left him hard and needy in his dreams.

The following morning, he took a break from his chapter to stock up on gingersnaps at the corner grocery store. Since he'd bought them expressly for Rose and her keeper, he was disappointed when they failed to show up later that day.

Or the day after that.

Or after that.

And when his writing once again turned as stale as the

cookies hardening into doorstops atop his kitchen counter, he was tempted to check into the retirement center next door to see if anything untoward had happened to the charming Mrs. Johansson—and her companion who had been acting as his unwitting writing muse.

Instead, he decided to do what Hemingway so often had done when feeling short on inspiration: he went back to the corner store and bought some whiskey to go with his fresh batch of gingersnaps.

Kayanne could feel the beginning of a migraine coming on. A mild twitching behind her right eye was working itself into a full-blown throb as she filled out yet another required piece of bureaucratic paperwork and counted the minutes until her shift would be over. Because they were so shorthanded at the center, she hadn't had a day off since her first day of working there. Between taking care of her ailing mother at home, adjusting to a new and decidedly unglamorous job, and fighting her craving for alcohol, she was feeling as brittle as a wishbone.

And just as likely to snap in two.

The last few days had been among the most trying of her life. Petulant photographers, vying divas and grueling hours under the most arduous of conditions were nothing compared to being treated like a recalcitrant teenager by her mother again.

Like a leper by old acquaintances.

And a sexual threat by a card-carrying member of AARP.

In between her mother's wheedling that she should find a good man with whom to settle down, her boss's lecherous perusal and overt disdain for their clients, and Rose's determination to get her fired, Kayanne found herself longing to wash away the indignities of life the old-fashioned way: with a bottle of tequila and shaker of salt.

It took an act of sheer willpower and commitment to the original twelve-step program to steer her past the nearest liquor store and into an AA meeting instead. Once a day she sought solace in the success stories of those who had been through it themselves—fellow drunks who neither stooped to condone excuses nor looked down upon her in judgment. Her sponsor, Bethany Moore, assured Kayanne that her present job at the Evening Star Retirement Manor was all part of a universal plan to assist in her recovery. Bethany believed that simple labor devoted to the good of others was exactly what an ex-model celebrity needed to learn proper humility. For her own part, Kayanne chalked it all up as karmic payback for her previous bad behavior.

Still, the day she'd received her six-month sobriety token, Kayanne had found the applause in that dingy, smoke-filled room warmer and far more genuine than the echoes of any star-studded event of her past.

Outside the four walls that bound her fellow AA members in blissful anonymity, life continued to present more challenges. Since her first successful break out, Rose Johansson was outdoing herself daily to repeat the feat. Tuesday she'd coerced a friend into calling the front desk with an elaborate story about scam artists targeting old-folks homes in hopes of distracting Kayanne long enough to slip out the front door unnoticed. Wednesday Rose had tried creeping unobtrusively behind a pile of laundry that had been leaving the building. When confronted, she had feigned confusion as convincingly as any legitimate Alzheimer's patient. But the next day when Kayanne had caught Rose climbing onto a chair placed strategically beneath her bedroom window, she'd dropped the innocent act and had proceeded to call her "warden" every name in the book.

It wasn't the kind of book Kayanne expected an old lady to check out of the library, either....

Claiming that an unruly five-year-old had nothing on Mrs. Johansson, J.R. had threatened to handcuff her to the bed if she kept up her shenanigans. Kayanne wasn't sure if her supervisor was joking or not. He didn't so much as bother to hide his contempt for the residents from anyone but visitors and potential clients. J.R. treated the elderly men and women who had raised families, owned businesses and fought in wars as though they were uncooperative children incapable of making even the simplest decision by themselves. His lack of people skills was partially responsible for the high turnover of staff at the Manor. The rest could be blamed on the atmosphere of impending death that permeated the place.

Despite her own reputation as a cold-hearted bitch, Kayanne couldn't bring herself to feel such detachment for the clients with whom she worked. Personally, she found them a good deal more interesting than J.R., who was apt to point out what a good catch he was whenever the opportunity presented itself. He was a man laboring under the delusion that his supervisory position more than made up for his lack of height and personality.

The way he looked at Kayanne made her skin crawl, but she did her best to shrug it off with a world-weariness that had yet to stoop her shoulders. If that little maggot thought he was going to use his influence to worm anything more than a cordial greeting from her, he would have to stand in line behind a long queue of men mistaken in their belief that they could use sex as a weapon against her.

Kayanne found herself absently wondering if Dave Evans was of the same ilk. Even though they'd only exchanged a few words in an awkward situation, he'd nonetheless made an impression on her. He'd been so sweet to Rose before Kayanne had put in an appearance that it was hard to think he'd have any ulterior motives along those lines. Of course, just because he was kind to old ladies didn't mean he was any different from J.R. in the way he treated younger ones. But as Rose was apt to point out, Dave certainly was easier on the eyes. And there was something about the man's quick smile that worked away at a girl's heart—even one as well protected as Kayanne's.

"Code ninety-nine."

A male voice over the intercom crackled with irritation. Code ninety-nine was the administration's secret way of informing workers that a resident was missing. While it didn't inspire the level of panic that such an announcement would have on Kayanne's first day at work, it was nonetheless the perfect culmination of a lousy week. She rubbed her temples. One didn't have to contact a psychic to figure out who was AWOL again.

Or where she was headed.

Dave couldn't have been more delighted when Rose dropped by looking as if she were dressed for a high tea than if the Queen of England had just announced her presence on his front stoop. Instead of the loose-fitting housedress that she'd worn the last time they'd met, today she was sporting a beige polyester pantsuit with a bright bow tied jauntily at her throat. Freshly set and colored, her hair was the same tint as the cotton candy he'd loved as a boy whenever the carnival had come to town.

"Where's your friend?" Dave asked, feigning nonchalance.

"That woman is not my friend," Rose said, taking the chair Dave offered her. "She is the bossiest, most controlling person I've ever had the displeasure to be around. You have no idea what I had to go through just to steal some time alone with you today."

Dave couldn't help but grin at the thought of Rose giving the indomitable Kayanne the slip. She didn't strike him as the sort who would enjoy playing hide-and-seek on her shift. He couldn't imagine why such a fascinating creature was hiding her beauty in, of all places, a retirement center, but he was determined to uncover the reason. As much as he wanted to believe that this budding obsession sprang only from a need to advance his own sluggish plot, he couldn't help but be enthralled with her as a person. And he wasn't fool enough to dismiss the physical attraction he felt for her as anything less than what it was.

Unmitigated lust.

He tried to look stern. "I hope this isn't another unauthorized visit, Rose."

She gave him an audacious wink that took him aback. "What Kayanne doesn't know won't hurt her."

"But it could very well hurt me," Dave replied, thinking about the many ways the redheaded drill sergeant could put him in his place. Some of which made his belly tighten.

He was in the process of looking up the number for the Evening Star Retirement Manor when Rose's keeper made a belated albeit not entirely unexpected appearance on his front porch.

"Isn't anyone going to invite me to the party?" she asked, sauntering up the walk and smiling at them both in a fashion reminiscent of the Cheshire cat from *Alice's Adventures in Wonderland.*

The way Kayanne managed to make a simple work smock look chic was worthy of at least a full page of description, Dave decided. She wasn't beautiful in the classical sense. More like Hilary Swank than the Grace Kelly type he was usually drawn to, Kayanne nevertheless had an aura about her that made a man take notice of the whole package. Tall, big boned and physically powerful, she wore sex like an exotic brand of perfume. Her hair had a windblown look that beckoned a man to run his fingers through it, looking for glints of gold among those fiery strands. There was nothing coy about the way she trained her piercing eyes on him either, tearing away his usual sense of ease and leaving him feeling exposed and guilty.

It was almost as if she knew the lascivious thoughts he'd been entertaining about her over the past few days.

Rose interrupted his runaway train of thought by snapping, "Everybody knows two's company and three's a crowd. Surely, Kayanne, you have more pressing issues back at the Manor than ruining my afternoon."

"I was just about to call," Dave interjected holding out the phone as if tendering a peace offering. "Would you care for a gingersnap and a drink?"

The flash of vulnerability he glimpsed in the depths of Kayanne's eyes was gone before she could arch a fine eyebrow into a question mark.

"Gingersnaps, huh?"

The look she gave him made him feel like the kind of scoundrel who might deliberately lure an old lady over to his place with cookies for the sole intention of getting to know her young companion better. Dave was surprised when she took a conciliatory stance and her mouth relaxed into a smile.

"I guess there's no reason for me to be a party pooper," she said, easing into the nearest chair.

Rose harrumphed. "Lordy, girl, don't you know how to take a hint?"

"Better than you apparently," Kayanne countered before turning her attention to Dave. "Houdini himself would have been easier to commandeer the last couple of days. I was afraid she was going to break a hip climbing out a window trying to sneak over here."

Dave did his best not to embarrass Rose by laughing. Here was the perfect opportunity to ask Kayanne for a date to see if he couldn't get to know her better. Preferably without her elderly client in tow. Figuring his chances would be greatly enhanced if he came across as a nice guy, he tried enlisting Rose as an ally and working his way up incrementally.

"I have an idea," he said. "Why don't you just set up a time every day when the two of you can come by to visit? That way Rose doesn't put herself in danger, you don't have to worry about her and everybody at the Manor can breathe a sigh of relief."

Kayanne studied him so intensely that Dave had to fight to keep from fidgeting.

"That sounds like a great idea," she said startling him by leaning in and deliberately invading his space. "There's just one thing I need to know before I go to my supervisor with this proposal."

"What's that?" Dave asked, doing his best neither to step back submissively nor to succumb to the desire to ravage her on the spot.

Kayanne gave him the kind of hard, searching look he suspected she reserved for men who were clearly after one thing and one thing alone.

"Just what's your angle, buddy?"

Three

Kayanne had slapped men who looked less shocked than Dave Evans did at the moment. Taking his indignation as a positive sign that he wasn't up to anything sneaky helped take the edge off any guilt she might feel for posing the question in the first place.

"Are you always so paranoid, or do I just bring that trait out in you?" Dave asked, all former charm wiped from his countenance.

Kayanne stopped overworking a piece of gum between her jaws to scowl at him.

"It's just you."

Rose harrumphed.

A smile toyed with the edges of Kayanne's lips. On some masochistic level she enjoyed matching wits with

Rose. It beat trying to coax a simple greeting from some of her other clients who were, as far as Kayanne was concerned, overmedicated and under-stimulated. She just hoped she was as stubborn and passionate as Rose when she reached eighty.

That Dave was serving the old lady's favorite cookie thawed something that had been frozen hard inside Kayanne for a long time. Recalling the wild escapades of her past, she wondered when she, of all people, had become the world's official rule enforcer instead of its number-one breaker. God surely had a wicked sense of humor.

Her mouth watered at the thought of washing away her troubles with a shot of something other than reality for a change.

"I'll take that glass of iced tea now," she said. "That is, if you're still offering."

There. Kayanne felt proud of herself for remaining on the wagon without anyone being the wiser about how incredibly difficult it had been not to ask for the "something stronger" Dave had offered the last time she'd been here. Her crusade was strictly personal in nature. She didn't feel the need to push her newfound sobriety on anyone else. Or expect the rest of the world to stop drinking just because she'd chosen sobriety over a lifestyle that had left her empty and used.

Of course, that didn't mean that she'd forgotten all about the old gang. She often found herself wondering what they were up to. And who her hard-drinking ex was spending his time with now that she was out of the picture.

Forrester would get quite a laugh out of seeing her in a shapeless smock working with a bunch of tired, old farts—a name he bestowed on anyone over the age of forty.

Forcibly pulling herself out of the past and into the present, Kayanne dialed the number for the retirement center.

"I've located Mrs. Johansson," she said. "There's no need to worry. She's safe and sound at a neighbor's less than a block away. As soon as she finishes up visiting here, we'll both be back."

With that, she disconnected and studied Dave at length while he fixed her drink. His dusty-blond hair was cut short in a tousled, no-nonsense style favored by athletes, and there was an outdoorsy air about him that belied the sedentary nature of his writing career. If he were to offer her a tour of the house, Kayanne bet she'd find one room devoted solely to weights and exercise equipment. She found it hard to believe he maintained that physique by lifting books alone.

It was difficult aligning his nice-guy image with the latent virility he emoted. Kayanne took a moment to examine her manicured nails. If she scratched beneath his courteous veneer, would she find a hot-blooded lover? Or just another loser out to get what he could from her?

"Are you from around here originally?" Dave asked, handing her a tall glass.

The slice of lemon decorating the rim was a nice touch, she thought.

"Born and raised right here in Sheridan County."

"You've lived here all your life then?"

While not inclined to go into details about her past, Kayanne saw no reason to avoid answering questions simply designed to facilitate polite conversation.

"I didn't say that. The truth is I couldn't get out of this provincial hellhole fast enough when I was younger."

"Feeling like that, what could have possibly brought you back here?"

"My mother had a heart attack, and she needs somebody to stay with her while she recuperates."

She felt no obligation to explain that the real reason she'd taken a break from modeling was to pull herself together. Or that her mother's illness had merely been the impetus to bring Kayanne back home rather than signing herself into a private rehab center that she could scarcely afford considering some of the terrible financial decisions she'd made at the height of her drinking.

"That's commendable," Dave said. "I understand about the need to get away from, and yet still stay connected to, family."

Kayanne caught the subtle lilt of a Southern drawl in his words. She wondered if it had been deliberately schooled out of him for the same reason her agent had encouraged her to lose her own Midwestern accent. He'd found it as hokey as the apple-pie name that her parents had given her.

Dave chatted on amiably unaware of the road her thoughts had taken. Charming, gracious and funny, he was attentive to Rose without being patronizing.

Shaking her head at his lame jokes, Kayanne found

herself truly relaxing for the first time in a long time that she could remember.

Without alcohol or drugs.

If she wasn't careful, she realized that she just might let her guard down. She forced herself to remember just how dangerous that could be to her sobriety. Holding Dave's gaze, she wondered how she might feel if it ever came down to breaking his heart. Undoubtedly a whole lot worse than in previous relationships with men like Forrester who didn't have hearts to break.

She glanced curiously at the laptop sitting open on the coffee table next to her.

"What are you writing, by the way?"

Dave feigned nonchalance as he reached across her to activate the screen saver. When his hand accidentally brushed across her arm, a frisson of awareness caused her to draw back as if she'd been scalded. Kayanne wondered if the unexpected tingles affecting her nerves were wreaking havoc with his as well.

"I already told you," Dave replied glibly, "the great American novel."

Having been around artistic types a good deal, Kayanne understood that novelists were territorial, but she couldn't imagine what—or who—this man thought he was protecting. Finding his response cliché and evasive, she didn't bother hiding her irritation.

"Surely you don't think either Rose or I are out to steal your ideas?"

Dave's smile wobbled at the corners. "Of course not.

It's just considered bad luck for a writer to show his work to anyone before he's had a chance to polish it."

Past experience led Kayanne to believe men would just as soon lie to your face as trust you with the truth on even the most inconsequential of matters. Not that she cared one way or the other. As long as it didn't involve her, she didn't give a damn what he wrote about. She suspected that, like so many of the *artistes* who'd frequented the same parties that she'd attended in New York, Dave hadn't produced much of anything other than empty bottles of booze. He was probably just embarrassed to be put on the spot.

"What do you like to read?" he asked, abruptly changing the subject.

Kayanne took a moment to respond. It wasn't the type of question often posed to her, she supposed because most people assumed she didn't read much. Actually, her tastes were quite eclectic. As a girl, she'd devoured just about anything she could get her hands on, and in high school, she'd discovered a fondness for the classics that her English teachers had forced upon their captive audiences. When her modeling career had been in full swing, she'd barely had time to skim the current fashion magazines. And since returning home, she hadn't picked up much because her mother's preference tended toward overtly religious themes that Kayanne found heavy-handed and oppressive.

"It depends," she answered. "If you've got anything on the shelf, I'd like to give you a read. What exactly is it you write?"

"It's been categorized as a combination between literary and dark fiction."

Once again she was irritated by the vagueness of his response. Dave Evans sounded very much like a professor. She imagined him wowing a classroom full of women with fabulous reviews of his work.

Feeling suddenly stupid, she ventured a question. "Just what kind of book isn't considered literary?"

Apparently one needed a college education to make such distinctions. Kayanne assumed that Dave would look down his nose at the popular fiction she enjoyed reading. She didn't have a lot of patience with snobs, having encountered her fair share of them who had associated her looks with a lack of intelligence. Especially when she'd been starting out as a green kid from the sticks.

"Kay Anne!" scoffed the first agent she'd approached. "If you're lucky, a sweet, little old name like that will get you about as far as the back door in this business. Sorry, kid, but I don't have the time to invest in trying to turn a desperate hick into a silk purse."

Even now the memory stung. Less than two years later she'd sent a copy of her first major magazine cover to the same fellow signed with her real name. After a painful trial-and-error period, Kayanne had discovered she could trick people into thinking she was chic by eliminating the space between her first and middle names, and adding a little *spice* to her country packaging.

"By literary," Dave explained, "I mean the kind of

books that usually generate great reviews but lousy royalties."

Kayanne smiled at his unexpected candor. That could explain why he needed to supplement his writing income by teaching.

Ever the capitalist, she ventured to ask, "Wouldn't it make sense to combine the two?"

"Good sense and inspiration don't always go together," Dave explained.

Belatedly remembering to include Rose in the conversation, Kayanne glanced over at the comfortable recliner the older woman had claimed as her throne. She was sound asleep. Dave and Kayanne shared a look akin to that of doting parents studying a sleeping infant. Granted, Rose didn't have the same cherubic face as a baby, but in repose she managed to pull off a look of innocence.

When a deep snore erupted from her lips, they laughed out loud.

Never had Kayanne felt so comfortable in the presence of such a drool-worthy man. Studying her surroundings, she decided his home reflected equal parts of industry and gentility. Books clearly held a place of importance in this house. They were neatly stacked from floor to ceiling in built-in bookcases, arranged artfully on the living room coffee table and littered in no apparent order about the recliner. A photograph of a handsome couple that Kayanne assumed were his parents rested on the mantel next to several of him in a variety of outdoor activities such as white-water rafting

CATHLEEN GALITZ   43

and skiing. It appeared that the American dream that had always been just out of reach for her when she'd been growing up poor and scared was this man's birthright.

She couldn't imagine him writing anything particularly dark. Maybe he was afraid of exploring the sinister aspects of his own personality and was thus drawn to such things in his imagination.

Or maybe, as in the fashion industry, dark themes were simply in vogue. More photographers than she cared to remember had tried making her into an angry, cruel beauty. Kayanne's athletic body and country-fresh face were contrary to the heroin addict's look so popular on Fifth Avenue. Even with a hangover, she'd had trouble pulling off Gothic. Her meteoric rise to the top of the industry had surprised almost everyone.

Her career was the last thing, however, she wanted to discuss with Dave. One of the nicest things about him was that he knew nothing about her past—neither the glamour that had set her apart nor the despair that had brought her back home.

"So how did you end up living at the brink of civilization as we know it?" she wanted to know.

"Unlike you, I deliberately picked it. I prefer Sheridan's sleepy streets and rugged mountains to Birmingham's botanical gardens and congestion."

"Does your family still live in Alabama?"

Dave's brow furrowed in consternation. "They're so entrenched in that generational soil that just getting them to visit is a terrible imposition. Like you, they don't understand what it is about the area that's such a magnet for me. They're hoping your bitter Wyoming winters will bring me to my senses."

He sounded suddenly sad, and Kayanne noticed how quickly he tried to change the subject away from himself.

"How long have you been working with the elderly?"

"About a week," she said with a trace of chagrin. "And if Rose doesn't start being a little more cooperative about staying put, I may not make it till my first payday."

Dave gave her a funny look. "Would that be so bad?"

He wasn't the only one who wondered if she was wasting her talents working at the Manor. Nevertheless, Kayanne was under no obligation to explain her reasons to anyone.

"Do you find something about my job to be beneath you?" she asked defensively.

Dave's response was immediate.

"The real question is whether it's beneath you. Forgive me for pointing out the obvious, but it seems strange that a woman as beautiful and intelligent as you would want to hide herself in a nursing home."

Kayanne was impressed by the fact that he somehow managed to flatter and insult her at the same time. As tempting as it might be to parade her accolades before him, it was even more refreshing to be taken at face value for a change. The truth of the matter was that it would suit her just fine if Dave Evans didn't find out about her past until well after she'd moved on with her future.

Kayanne was saved from having to come up with a clever response by another loud snore, one that actually shook Rose awake. Looking embarrassed, she wiped a spot of drool off her chin.

"I hope you enjoyed your little catnap," Dave said with a reassuring smile meant to ease her mind.

"I did, thank you. Now, if you don't mind, Kayanne dear, I'm ready to go home."

Kayanne assumed that the endearment was more for Dave's benefit than generated from any genuine fondness toward her, but she was happy to oblige nonetheless. Sitting in this sunny little nook drinking iced tea was making her sappy. She saw little point in wishing for the kind of life that had been denied her. God knows her widowed mother had done the best she could to provide, and if their home lacked the warmth of this man's at least she'd never gone hungry.

At least not physically.

"You'll be sure to come back, won't you?" Dave asked as he escorted them to the front door.

Rose didn't hesitate. "Of course."

"I'll see what the boss has to say about it." That was all Kayanne would commit to. She had all she could manage trying to survive day by day without a drink without cluttering up her life with social obligations.

She helped Rose slowly down the porch steps and stopped to let her rest at the bottom. There Kayanne studied Dave as if considering whether to divulge a state secret of the gravest importance.

"Romantica," she blurted out.

When he looked at her quizzically, she gave him a grin that completely undermined the tough-girl image she'd worked so hard to perfect. It delighted her to know a little something about the publishing industry that he didn't.

"That's what I like to read."

Four

Dave had to look up *romantica* on the Internet to find out exactly what it was. A cross between romance and erotica, the description alone whetted his interest—in the enigmatic woman who'd claimed to read it as well as the genre itself. He'd never met anyone more intriguing. It hadn't escaped his notice that Kayanne didn't like talking about herself and her past. As mysterious as the waxing and waning moon, she was lighting his way through a book that was miraculously getting easier to write every day. Although Dave couldn't honestly say that he found her altogether up to the standards of gentility and charm that he usually applied to his heroines, he couldn't deny that he wanted her, either.

Just the word *romantica* conjured up images of Kayanne lying naked in bed beneath him. Ashamed that he didn't have better control over his thoughts, Dave reminded himself that her disclosure about being a closet romantic didn't bode well for turning their relationship into something of a more passionate nature. As much as he'd like to believe the lady was into fleeting sexual gratification, her choice of reading material indicated otherwise. Whether she'd ever admit to it or not, Dave suspected Kayanne was looking for a long-term commitment—just like every other woman he knew. And the only commitment he was willing to make at the moment was to his writing.

Given Kayanne's reading preferences, he doubted if she would be much impressed with what he wrote. He imagined that she would find it as pretentious as he did on those days when he was feeling most vulnerable. How ironic that his literary awards left him feeling such a fraud. Afraid that he wouldn't be able to repeat his initial literary success, he'd wrestled with self-doubt that had manifested itself in a full-blown case of writer's block.

Dave had no idea how Kayanne's unexpected presence allowed him to sidestep that block. He simply knew that she was able to blast through it with those piercing green eyes of hers as if she were endowed with superhuman powers. As disconcerting as it might be to have her alter ego Spice take over the page without even bothering to let him know what she was up to, Dave preferred chasing her on a wild ride to staring at a blank screen wondering if the only way to prime his creative pump was with a stiff drink.

If he failed to meet his looming deadline and produce something at least as good if not better than his debut novel, he would ultimately have to admit that his parents were right and do what they'd wanted him to do all along: give up his dream of writing and come home to fulfill his destiny of taking over the family business. He had no desire to spend the rest of his life litigating other people's miseries as part of the firm of Evans, Evans and—soon to be—Evans. Unfortunately his feelings on the matter were beside the point. If he couldn't turn his writing into something more lucrative and less excruciating, he'd have little choice but to support himself with his teaching job. And while that might be an acceptable option for someone raised with a lower standard of living, he'd grown up with expensive tastes. Dave couldn't imagine struggling to meet the rent every month.

The only thing more untenable would be having to sponge off his parents.

Kayanne had no idea that she was responsible for postponing his career crisis a little while longer. And while it was true that he had lost control of his plot since she'd waltzed into his life, he was happy to be writing fluently again—without feeling the compulsion to edit every single word until little but soup was left. Writing had become fun again. And in spite of his critics' stuffy literary expectations, an element of mystery and romantica was seeping into his book.

Convincing J.R. to sanction Rose's expeditions to Dave's house wasn't nearly as difficult as Kayanne had first imagined. As much grief as the old lady had caused the entire staff the past few days, everybody was eager to accommodate her insomuch as it kept them from having to clamp a police-issued monitor on her ankle or hire a full-time bodyguard to watch over her. If all it took to keep Mrs. Johansson from being forcibly detained was giving her a little time to visit a willing neighbor, then J.R. was all for it.

These outings perked Rose up like a parched flower beneath a welcome rain shower. So immediate and obvious was her transformation that other residents began taking notice. Some wanted to know what kind of elixir she was taking. Others wanted directions to the fountain of youth from her.

"It's right across the street," Rose replied coyly.

The special attention she'd started paying her hair and makeup, however, did little to improve on a wardrobe she claimed was "as outdated as the Depression." As much as Kayanne hated to agree, she was of the opinion that the contents of Rose's entire closet should be donated to the nearest Goodwill store.

"Would you mind taking me shopping today?" Rose asked, feigning a sweetness that Kayanne knew she only employed when she wanted someone to do something for her—or she was trying to impress Dave.

"And don't worry about money. It's not an issue. For all intents and purposes, I'm loaded. I'd just like to buy a few things that don't make me feel ready to fall into a casket."

Delighted at the prospect of escaping the dreariness

of the retirement center, Kayanne obtained permission to take Rose shopping and was relieved to discover that she hadn't exaggerated her financial situation. Kayanne had mistakenly assumed that most of the residents at Evening Star were there under the auspices of Medicare or Medicaid. For many, health issues, not finances, were the reason they resided at the retirement center.

That made her feel a whole lot more comfortable parking a company vehicle in front of a trendy boutique rather than a discount store where the quality of garments was considerably below her high standards. Ultimately though, style ended up proving to be more a problem than price. Kayanne hadn't realized the dearth of stylish clothes available for older women. Colors ranged from beige to navy to black, and it seemed that everything, including pants, blouses and dresses, was cut in boxy, shapeless styles that even mannequins couldn't manage to make look good.

Steering Rose into a younger section didn't help either. There, the trends gravitated to extremes, the choices being between streetwalker wear and frilly outfits suitable for prom.

"May I help you find something?" the salesclerk inquired.

"How about something in between the prosti-tot section and the coroner's corner?" Kayanne suggested candidly.

If the old saying that a designer is only as good as his last collection was true, Kayanne thought whoever was responsible for the hideous clothes they waded through all afternoon deserved to be run out of the business. The problem wasn't store specific she discovered as they perused other boutiques. That the hyper-competitive business of selling clothes completely overlooked one lucrative demographic blew Kayanne away.

And planted a seed in her mind.

With her experience and knowledge of the fashion industry, it wouldn't be an insurmountable leap from modeling clothes to designing them. If she was ever into big money again, Kayanne thought designing for the mature market might be something worth pursuing.

For the moment, however, she settled for mixing and matching accent pieces from the younger section with a few core pieces from the more matronly racks.

Rose was delighted. "I feel seventy all over again!" she exclaimed.

So pleased was she in fact that she didn't even fall asleep in the middle of her next visit with Dave as she usually did.

"My, don't you look particularly pretty today," he said, opening the door to let her in.

Although Rose was the only one to blush, the compliment pleased both her and Kayanne. As trying as their little shopping trip had proven in some ways, it beat the heck out of Kayanne's tedious routine of dispensing pills and adjusting television screens at the home. Shopping without a budget had stirred in her an innate love of fashion.

"Maybe you should consider a career in the industry," Dave suggested after listening to Rose describe in detail Kayanne's genius with textures, colors and fabrics.

Kayanne gave him a hard look to see if he was making fun of her. She wouldn't be surprised if he hadn't already heard from any number of people about her ignominious fall from the heights of Manhattan to her present status. Seeing no sign of ridicule in his features, she decided to take the comment at face value.

"I've thought about it a time or two before," she said with an edge of self-reproof that went right over his head.

Rose was less obtuse. "Let me know when you decide to market those fashion skills of yours," she said. "I'm always willing to back a good idea when it's coupled with an architect to see it through completion."

Later that week, Kayanne was flattered once again when some of the other female residents approached her and asked if she would consider helping them spruce up, too. Kayanne decided that her AA sponsor might be on to something about serving others being good for the soul. Hard work and involvement in other people's lives actually did seem to be curbing her appetite for alcohol.

Rose's comment got her thinking about blending her newfound sense of service with a career for which she was more suited. Modeling hardly prepared a girl for the grind of working in an old folks' home. And a future in nursing held as much appeal to someone of her temperament as starting up her own convent—although she figured she might just as well nominate herself Sister Superior and christen the order the Sisters of Perpetual Atonement. That Dave Evans kept popping into her head on such a regular basis lately seemed sure proof that she'd been celibate far too long. Linking sobriety to a life without men, she didn't see things improving in that area of her life any time soon though.

Her mother had other ideas about her self-imposed state of chastity. Having finally recuperated enough to start bossing her daughter around again, Suzanne Aldarmann had resumed nagging where she'd left off years ago. She'd started by informing Kayanne it was time to settle down and start producing a grandchild for her. As soon as possible.

Finally, after enduring as much badgering as she could stand, Kayanne asked her point-blank, "Do you remember that part of why I left here in the first place was because of you constantly interfering in my life, Mom?"

"Now that wasn't the only reason, dear."

A deeply religious woman, Kayanne's mother had a penchant for belaboring the past. Not that anyone could blame her. Her life had been hard—she'd lost her husband prematurely to cancer, had raised a headstrong child single-handedly on waitress wages and had dealt with serious health issues herself. Still, since reliance on a man hadn't prepared her mother to live independently, it confounded Kayanne that Suzanne's solution to everything wrong in her daughter's life was marriage.

"If you're so sold on the institution, why don't you quit pestering me and find a nice man yourself?"

Her mother's long-suffering sigh spoke volumes. "You of all people should know that no one could ever replace your father."

Kayanne bit her tongue. The truth of the matter was that she could remember little about her father except the ruthlessness of the illness that had ravaged his once strong body. What she remembered most was the terrible, traumatizing pain of losing him. At eight years old, Kayanne had felt more anger than grief at being thus abandoned. Even at that tender age, she had been willful. More often than not her father had had to step forward to intervene as the mediator between his wife and daughter. Once he was gone, the battle to conquer Kayanne's spirit had begun in earnest.

It was a war Suzanne had been destined to lose. One that had prepared Kayanne for the many skirmishes to follow in a business that devoured the faint of heart.

"Is it so much to ask for grandchildren to bring some joy to my twilight years?" Suzanne asked with a martyr's wringing of the hands.

"They'd be sure to be just as much trouble as I was, Mom," Kayanne assured her. "And at your age, I'm not sure your heart could stand that much mayhem."

What with her mother's badgering, the dearth of shopping and constant reminders of a sad childhood all around, it didn't take Kayanne long to recollect why she'd been so eager to shake the dust of this town's streets off her shoes a decade ago and make a place for herself in the world beyond. Aside from its picturesque mountains and crystal-clear skies, there was little to do in this sleepy little town. Except party.

Considering that the museum listed itself as Sheridan's number-one attraction, it was a given that opportunities abounded for illicit activities. Here, teenagers explored their budding sexuality in the backseats of cars parked at the same drive-in theater that Kayanne had frequented in her youth. And the soaring price of gas hadn't deterred anyone from "hanging Main" as a primary form of entertainment, either.

It was little wonder that young people were leaving the community as fast as they could get a diploma in their hot little hands. Kayanne still felt guilty about abandoning her mother the instant she was out of high school. And she worried how Suzanne was going to manage when she left again. Even if there were some way of better utilizing her talents in this backwater setting, she wasn't sure she would want to relocate here anyway.

With so little of interest to do in her spare time Kayanne began doodling clothing designs. With her connections, it wouldn't be all that difficult to find the right fabrics and locate seamstresses who could bring her ideas to life.

"Would you mind helping me wash my hair, dear?" Suzanne asked.

Kayanne acquiesced to one of her least favorite chores without a word of complaint. Whatever her problems with her mother, she refused to let them get in the way of her duties as a daughter. She placed a chair in front of the kitchen sink and positioned Suzanne on it as comfortably as possible. Since her mother was still weak from her surgery, it was difficult to bend her head over the sink without hurting her in the process.

"Make sure the water's not too hot. Last time you scalded me."

"I'm sorry, Mom."

Kayanne tested the temperature with her elbow, then wet her mother's hair. Lathering a dab of golden shampoo in her hands, she recalled how she'd started drinking as a way of initiating herself into the popular crowd and escaping the dreariness of living in a home where nothing she ever did was right. She pressed the trigger of the spray nozzle attached to the faucet and cleared all the cold water from it before directing the flow to Suzanne's head.

"Try to lean back a little farther," Kayanne prompted, trying to avoid drizzling water down Suzanne's collar.

After what she'd put her mother through during her turbulent adolescent years, Kayanne considered her present servitude a fair penance. She only wished she could wash away some of those painful memories as easily as the strands of hair swirling in the white enamel sink. Her mother blamed Kayanne for putting the gray in her hair with her underage drinking and high-spirited shenanigans.

Coming from a wide-open state where the miles between towns were measured by six-packs and bottles of booze, Kayanne herself had been surprised how ill-prepared she'd been for the level of substance use that she'd encountered in the city. She counted herself lucky that she'd never been drawn to putting anything up her nose or directly into her veins. All she'd needed to anesthetize herself to the stresses of her career and personal life was good old-fashioned legal alcohol.

Forrester was one of the few people Kayanne had ever met who could literally drink her under the table.

It had been while she was with him that her own drinking had spiraled out of control. Right up until the moment he crossed the line between having a good time and being downright mean, Forrester was one of the most fun people in the world to be with. But when his hard drinking had led to hard-fisted blows, Kayanne knew she had to make a choice. Showing up for a gig sporting a black eye and bruised ribs was considered in poor taste for a swimsuit edition. No masochist who needed daily beatings to figure out something was wrong, Kayanne had left after the first incident.

And had begged Forrester from a distance to make a change.

He had, in record time, by promising to transform himself into a better man—all the while sneaking around behind her back with one of her "closest" friends. Given a history of such disastrous relationships, it was little wonder Kayanne had come to associate hitting rock bottom with men in general. She'd dated so many guys who lived on the edge that it was hard to separate healthy relationships from unhealthy ones.

"Ouch!"

Her mother bolted upright in the chair, knocking her head on the back of the sink in the process.

"Pay attention to what you're doing. While you were off daydreaming somewhere, I got soap in my eyes," Suzanne complained.

She would have none of her daughter's profuse apologies. Grabbing the towel out of Kayanne's hands, Suzanne dripped water on the floor while attempting to wipe the offending soap from her eye. After cleaning up the mess, Kayanne offered to set her mother's hair for her even though she hated the thought of it—working with hair was absolutely repugnant. Especially her mother's, which was thin and attached to what had to be the most sensitive scalp on the planet.

She gathered up the same pink sponge curlers she remembered from high school and started rolling her mother's hair into neat rows. Kayanne did her best to keep her mind on the task at hand but couldn't help her thoughts wandering to Dave Evans. For some reason, she wondered what kind of a drunk Dave Evans was. Was he mean? Or the sloppy, sentimental sort who liked to toss obscure verse around in hopes of impressing the barflies with his academic credentials? It was hard to imagine him inebriated. Come to think of it, since the first time they'd met, she hadn't seen any sign of the whiskey bottle she'd spotted on his porch.

The ringing phone caused her mother to jump again and Kayanne to pull her hair.

"Answer that, would you?" Suzanne said, rubbing her scalp.

"I wish you'd let me buy you a caller identification box or answering machine so you could screen your calls," Kayanne told her. "I hate being bothered by salespeople when I'm in the middle of something."

"Those contraptions are a waste of money," Suzanne replied.

Kayanne knew that bringing such "modern technology" into the house would only lead to an argument about how much money she'd sent home over the years and what had become of it. So she simply did as she was told and picked up the receiver. If there had been any way to know who the caller was in advance, she definitely would have let the phone ring off the hook rather than take a call destined to suck her even deeper into the mire of the past.

Five

Jasmine was dead. Someone dashed her brains out with a blunt object and left her bleeding all over page seventy-eight. The viciousness of the crime shocked Dave—and, on some visceral level, fascinated him as well. While he couldn't prove anything, he secretly suspected Spice, who had never made any bones about her antipathy for cool, submissive blondes with nothing between their ears but outdated moral platitudes.

Poor, beautiful Jasmine. Cut down in the prime of her youth before being given the opportunity to consummate her one great love. Dave wondered why anyone would want to kill someone so perfect. His grieving process was cut short by morbid curiosity however. He believed a certain fiery redhead had all the answers, but she wasn't talking.

Unusually tight-lipped and evasive, Spice had taken to parading a stream of incongruous lovers across the pages of a novel that suddenly seemed to be writing itself. Dave suspected her scandalous behavior was designed more as a shock tactic to throw him off the trail than from any sensual pleasure derived behind closed doors. Confused and a little jealous, Dave knew the place to dig for answers was in the real world outside his imagination.

He looked forward to Rose's and Kayanne's visits insomuch as they provided the necessary creative fuel for him to keep writing at such an accelerated pace. They also were a pleasure in and of themselves. He wished there was some way to swing an actual date with Kayanne so he could delve the depths of her personality.

While not as intimidating as the character she had spawned in his book, like Spice, there was an edge to Kayanne that cut through anything that smacked of pretense. Dave found that refreshing. He also admired her wry sense of humor and a quick wit that wouldn't let him get away with a thing. Hence he made a point of shutting down his computer whenever she was around. He wasn't nearly as worried about the threat of libel for "borrowing" from real life as he was afraid that Kayanne might feel personally betrayed if she were ever to identify herself in the thickening plot.

The sound of the doorbell prompted him to close his laptop, leaving no telltale sign of the liberties he was taking with Kayanne's life. Having never seen her in anything other than her work-issued uniform, Dave wondered what she would look like in the same thing

Spice was wearing in the scene he was presently writing. That is, in nothing at all.

Although he was expecting both Rose and her keeper, he didn't think he ever could get used to the way Kayanne changed the molecular structure of the air itself whenever she entered a room. Opening the door of his home to her was like letting fresh air into a stuffy library.

"Come on in, sunshine," he said, taking Rose by the elbow and helping her to the chair from which she held forth like a queen surrounded by her loyal subjects.

Kayanne seemed particularly fidgety today and couldn't be coaxed into sitting down. While Dave and Rose discussed various issues of the day, Kayanne meandered around the room inspecting various mementos: photographs and paintings, an eclectic collection of antiques, a western bronze and a couple of framed awards for his writing. When she tested a glass paperweight in one hand, Dave couldn't help but think about how it was heavy enough to crack a person's skull if hurled with enough force....

"I looked for your novel at the local bookstore," she mentioned in a tone best described as noncommittal. "There weren't any copies available."

That came as no surprise. The typical shelf life of a book was slightly little longer than a carton of yogurt, and much of the space in typical stores was allocated to only the biggest names in the industry. Dave's dream was to someday be among them.

"If you'd like, I'll sign one for you out of my personal stash," he offered.

The conflict that played upon Kayanne's features left little doubt that she hated feeling indebted to anyone for anything. Even something as trifling as a book.

"That won't be necessary. I had them order one for me."

Dave was slightly relieved. How would he have signed such a gift anyway?

With love?

Hot for you?

Thanks for contributing without consent to my next book....

"It should be in sometime soon," Kayanne said. "I told them they should buy at least a gross once school starts and all your soon-to-be adoring students meet you in person."

Dave gave her a funny look. Could it be possible that such a stunning woman was actually exhibiting signs of jealousy?

Her usual presumptuous self, Rose didn't hesitate inserting herself into the conversation. "Personally *I'd* love one of your books."

He smiled. "I like a woman who knows what she wants," he said, leaving the room with the promise that he'd be right back. When he returned a moment later, he was carrying a book.

"Hardback," Kayanne observed. "Impressive."

Dave handed it to Rose who clutched it to her bosom as though it were the Holy Grail itself.

"I'll cherish it forever," she gurgled, opening it to the inscription and reading it out loud. "To my dear friend,

Rose. Fondly from your next-door neighbor and admirer, Dave Evans."

Rose dabbed at her eyes with a frilly handkerchief. "I hope you know how fond I am of you, too, dear."

Kayanne was impressed. It was the perfect dedication. Thoughtful and tender without being overtly sappy. While Dave and Rose carried on a friendly conversation about literature, Kayanne sauntered over to the front window and considered the world outside this pleasant sanctuary. A harbinger of change in the air, a slight breeze rustled the tops of a stand of aspen trees. Lost in reflection about the phone call that had left her feeling so utterly vulnerable, Kayanne was startled when Dave came up behind her a little while later to share the view.

He put a gentle hand on her shoulder. "I didn't mean to scare you," he said.

Despite the intent, his touch was not in the least reassuring. It had been such a long time since she'd felt a man's hands upon her that Kayanne longed to direct them over every inch of her body. Or at the very least to lean into his hard masculinity and turn that touch into something more substantial—such as a full-fledged embrace.

Kayanne wondered what it would be like to let herself lean on someone strong. Someone who wasn't out to use her. Someone around whom she could let down her guard and share the dream of a normal life. Images of creating a home of her own with someone special flashed through her mind and left her feeling conflicted.

"Rose has nodded off," Dave said.

Turning to face him directly, Kayanne saw that the

warmth of his touch matched the heat of his gaze. Seeing herself reflected in eyes the color of melted chocolate, she caught a glimpse of a woman without a past. And couldn't help but fantasize for a fleeting instant about wrapping herself around this man and pretending to be exactly what he needed. Dave was so sweet that she hesitated inviting him into a world colored by cynicism and hard experience. Having worked so hard to overcome the shortcomings of her youth, Kayanne hated the thought of losing control of the image she'd fashioned for herself, whether as a top fashion model or as a woman doing her best to get her life back together.

The words she'd practiced stuck sideways in her throat.

"I have to ask you a favor."

Amusement toyed with the corners of his sensual, masculine mouth. "It must be something terrible to make you tremble so," Dave pointed out.

That he'd even noticed said a lot about his sensitivity. When he took her hands in his, it only intensified the tremors that had taken over Kayanne's body. Once again, she was rendered helpless by the charge of pure sexual energy sizzling between them. Blood poured through her veins like hot brandy.

Kayanne reminded herself that there were always repercussions in asking a favor from any man. Although Dave didn't strike her as the sort who might expect something sexual in return, she still hated risking their tenuous friendship. However accidental in nature it might be, Dave was the only male in town she counted as a friend.

"What kind of favor?" he asked.

Her sponsor had insisted that it was time to stop dancing around the past and confront it once and for all. Bethany seemed convinced this opportunity was God Himself knocking on her front door.

Kayanne wasn't so sure.

"I know it's terribly late to ask," she said in a rush. "But my class reunion is coming up this weekend, and I was wondering if you would mind going with me?"

"That's all?"

Dave sounded incredulous. His smile alone lifted the heavy weight pressing on Kayanne's chest.

"I thought you were going to ask me for a kidney or something even more dear."

"I wouldn't take bets on which would be more painful," she told him in all honesty.

He threw back his head and laughed at her candor. "I'd love to go. But before I commit myself to a night of such impending doom, I have to ask. Why go at all if you don't want to?"

It was a fair question. And the same one she had been asking herself ever since she'd received the call from a former classmate informing her that her old mentor Mrs. Rawlins was going to be honored with special recognition Saturday night and had specifically requested that Kayanne be present.

"It has to do with being there for a lady who was there for me when I was young and confused," she said, chewing her lower lip in consternation. "And with making amends."

To an entire town...

Watching Dave's reaction closely to see what effect that admission would have upon him, she wondered if his writer's training helped him remain so stoic. Or if he simply had no idea that her reference came straight out of AA's big book.

"I'm hoping to save time and money hunting down everybody I've offended," she explained, donning a cavalier attitude. "This way I should be able to catch most of them in one place and get it over with all at once."

Her fellow alcoholics reassured Kayanne that this business of making amends was key to a successful recovery. It was hard arguing with their collective victories. Having failed miserably at white-knuckled sobriety before, she couldn't allow pride and tricky step number nine to be all that came between her and serenity.

"In that case, I'd be honored."

Kayanne let out the lungful of air that she'd been holding on to. Pertinent information regarding the date and time came out in a whoosh of exhalation. Feeling suddenly light-headed, she swayed on boneless legs.

Dave reached out to steady her. His efforts had completely the opposite effect. Falling against him, she felt the length of his hard body as he enveloped her in his arms. Like a desert nomad finding respite in the shade of an oasis, she took safe haven in the protection of a pair of strong and gentle arms.

Minute details leaped out at her. Gold flecks in his kind, dark eyes. Laugh lines around his sexy mouth. The closeness of his shave. A subtle hint of cologne almost masked by the clean scent of soap. Kayanne wondered vaguely how Dave always managed to look as if he'd just stepped out of the shower. In spite of her determination to keep their relationship on a platonic level, she found herself willing him to kiss her!

Kayanne wondered how some women could live without sex and feel blessed when others like herself considered celibacy a curse. In her own case, she saw it a necessary measure for maintaining sobriety. Passionate by nature, she didn't know which was worse: going without alcohol or going without sex for the rest of her life.

Testing the powers of her own resistance, she told herself that one little kiss was far different than one little drink.

She closed her eyes and leaned into the kiss they'd both been wanting since first laying eyes on one another. Threading her fingers into the short hair at the nape of his neck, she pulled Dave's mouth down to hers. His lips were firm, his response as hungry as her own. There was nothing tentative in his reaction as he took control, demanding everything she had to give.

Writhing with the intensity of the pleasure that rolled through her, Kayanne melted against him and marveled at the wonder of tasting a man without alcohol on his breath. It was far more intoxicating than she could have ever imagined.

Never had she experienced such a powerful reaction to a simple kiss. A simple tongue-tangling, high-voltage, soul-merging kiss that made her want to rip off his shirt and drag him to the nearest bedroom. The air around them crackled with enough sexual current to light up the entire state during a full-scale blackout.

Behind them someone cleared her throat.

They separated as quickly as a pair of teenagers caught necking in the back seat of a car by the local police.

"I'm having some palpitations. Would you mind taking me home right away?" Rose asked in a weak voice.

Her hand fluttered delicately toward her heart as she glared a hole straight through Kayanne, who was clearly the sole object of her fury. A typical clueless male, Dave seemed unaware that Rose felt anything other than the actual fondness she professed for him. As understandable as that was given the difference in their ages, Kayanne couldn't help but feel sorry for Rose.

And a tiny bit frightened for herself.

She acquiesced to "Her Majesty's" command with all the expediency demanded of an impending heart attack. Even though technically she'd done nothing wrong, Kayanne hadn't meant to hurt the old lady's feelings. Nor did she want to be responsible for causing her cardiac arrest either.

"Do you want me to call an ambulance?" she asked.

"I'll be just fine," Rose said icily.

All her life it seemed Kayanne had been destined to hurt those she cared for the most. Some people actually claimed that her love was as deadly as poison, a charge that she knew could very well be repeated at the reunion by some of her old classmates. In the past, Kayanne supposed she'd been subconsciously drawn to men whose appeal didn't go beyond the physical for fear of endangering anyone she really loved.

A shrink would have a heyday with her neuroses.

Rose suffered no such psychological preconceptions. She knew exactly who she was mad at. And why. Kayanne supposed it was a tribute to her upbringing as a lady that the octogenarian waited until they safely cleared the front gate before turning on her.

"Why, you backstabbing little bitch!"

Six

A few short weeks ago, all Kayanne would have been worried about was how to get Rose safely back to the retirement home without compromising her job in the process. Today, her heart was on the line. Decidedly uncomfortable with being the object of the old lady's ire, she tried teasing her way back into Rose's good graces.

"For someone with heart palpitations you sure are setting quite a pace today."

Anger took all the shuffle out of Rose's feet as she made a beeline to the pedestrian crossing. Kayanne had to double her stride just to keep up.

"I pity the poor Boy Scout who tries to take your arm to help you across this street," she joked.

"And I pity the Girl Scout who puts her trust in you!" Rose spat without bothering to slow down.

"I didn't mean to hurt you," Kayanne said, addressing the pain behind that statement. "It just happened. Besides, weren't you the one who encouraged me to explore all Dave's good traits and give him a chance?"

"I didn't intend for you to give him a tonsillectomy," Rose shrieked. "I can't believe that I actually thought you were my friend."

"I am," Kayanne said, wishing there was some way to prove it.

Seeing how the old lady was in no mood for a reasonable analysis of the situation, Kayanne counted herself lucky to escape the wide swing of her purple cane. What she really needed was an alternate plan to divert Rose's attention from the crisis at hand.

"What d'ya say we work on finding you a more…" Kayanne trailed off, wanting to find just the right word. "Age-appropriate suitor."

Rose brushed off the suggestion. "I have a better idea," she huffed. "Instead of trying to line me up with somebody from the mortuary, why don't you just stay the hell away from me!"

Getting Rose settled in her room after that was about as easy as directing an angry wasp into its nest. Kayanne fretted throughout the remainder of her shift, racking her brains for somebody worthy of Rose's interest. Until she could locate the lucky fellow, however, she vowed to do exactly what Rose had asked of her and keep her distance.

Rose might not be speaking to her, but Kayanne's

mother was more than happy to fill that void. She hadn't been able to stop talking since hearing that her daughter had a bona fide date with the most eligible bachelor in town—a man who wasn't going to arrive at the front door with a motorcycle helmet and matching attitude tucked in the crook of his arm. Whenever Kayanne had the opportunity to get a word in edgewise, she warned her mother not to get her hopes up about anything long-term developing with Dave.

Asking Dave to be her date had been a calculated risk on her part. Kayanne's standard approach to dating was to use men before they could use her. It was a strategy borne out of a painful string of doomed relationships intended to satisfy the libido without engaging the heart. Even now she could think of any number of men who would be glad for an excuse to help her live up to—or down—the community's expectations. There was something particularly gratifying about the thought of showing up at the reunion with the most desirable single man in town on her arm. Something comforting about having Dave at her side as she navigated the dangerous waters of her past.

Kayanne knew this event was sure to be a test of her recent sobriety. She assumed at least one *kind* soul would feel the need to take pity on Dave by helping him rectify the mistake he'd made in agreeing to be her date. Old rumors were sure to be embellished and exaggerated. Old wounds were likely to be ripped open anew. And liquor was sure to flow.

Kayanne knew that Dave was bound to hear negative

things about her sooner or later, and there wasn't a thing she could do about that. According to the precepts of AA, all she could do was to sweep her side of the walk and hope the people to whom she owed amends did the same.

It was just too bad that wasn't as easy to put into practice as it sounded in the safety of anonymity and unconditional friendship.

The day of the class reunion arrived in blistering heat, but by evening the temperature in the mountain town dropped to a cool fifty degrees. Kayanne considered the weather a precursor of the reception she could expect to receive from her old classmates. Extreme swings of climate. There was a lot of old baggage waiting for her behind those high-school doors, and the closer it came for the time for Dave to pick her up, the more she regretted her decision to go at all.

As far back as junior high school, Kayanne remembered being embarrassed by her circumstances. Sheridan, Wyoming, might be considered the boonies by cosmopolitan standards, but there was plenty of old wealth piled behind lodgepole archways of immense ranches and the doors of merchants whose families had made their fortunes generations ago. More recently, technology allowed CEOs and independently wealthy entrepreneurs from all over the country to move into the idyllic, isolated settings where businesses could be run long-distance via an Internet connection. Kayanne found it amusing to witness the clash of old and new money in ostentatious contests where polo competed with rodeo on summer weekends as the town's favored pastime.

As a girl, she hadn't had enough familiarity with prosperity to understand that all communities had snobbish elements. She simply had never felt good enough in a system that had pandered to children living with both biological parents and enough money not to have to shop at the Salvation Army for clothes. And just as she had all those years ago growing up under the shadow of the Big Horn Mountains and a pervasive sense of deprivation, Kayanne felt ashamed of being ashamed all over again.

Everything considered, the trailer where she'd grown up had been tidy and well kept. Her mother had more than met her obligation of putting a roof over her daughter's head and food on the table. Still, cruel comments about "trailer-park trash" stung to this day.

That Kayanne had been invited to the most exclusive parties in the world as an adult was somehow eclipsed by the fact that she'd been excluded from certain birthday parties as a child because she couldn't afford a nice enough present to warrant the price of admission. And as hard as Kayanne was working on overcoming the stubborn pride that proved to be an obstacle to her sobriety, she couldn't help but take some satisfaction in the fact that she would be wearing a designer original gown tonight.

Understated in its simplicity, the black Versace halter-top dress she'd chosen for the occasion hugged her figure and emphasized her curves. Slits on either side allowed a tantalizing hint of those often-photographed shapely legs, and a seethrough wrap bedecked with tiny seed pearls provided a false impression of modesty. A triad of diamonds representing the past, present and future glittered from a gold chain resting between her breasts.

Kayanne may have looked like packaged dynamite, but on the inside she felt every bit as awkward and unworthy as she had in high school. She didn't need a shrink to tell her that the obscenely expensive dress was her way of masking old insecurities. She only wished there was as easy a way to camouflage her home. There was little to be done to spruce up the trailer beyond buying a bouquet of fresh flowers to make the front room look less drab. And less like a shrine to cheap, sentimental knickknacks.

It infuriated Kayanne that her mother hadn't used the money that she'd sent when she was commanding top dollar in her field to do what she'd asked her to do: buy a beautiful home in an affluent neighborhood and fill it with all the lovely things her mother deserved.

"I've lived in this trailer for almost thirty years, and I intend to die here," was all Suzanne Aldarmann had had to say on the matter.

There was no arguing with such logic. When Kayanne had followed up with questions about living expenses, her mother had politely thanked her for providing enough to take care of the outrageous medical expenses. That had to be worth something, Kayanne supposed. Still, she wished her mother had stashed enough away to carry her ever-irresponsible daughter through the hard times she was presently going through. She suspected some slick preacher had preyed on Suzanne's conscience and bamboozled her out of most of the money Kayanne had sent her.

Grateful to count this humble abode a sanctuary while she struggled to get back on her feet, Kayanne tamped down any shame she might feel about Dave having to pick her up here. She told herself that she didn't have to impress anybody at this point in her life.

Why then, Kayanne wondered, was she so nervous hearing the knock at the front door?

"Wow!"

Although she knew that anything she wore tonight had to be an improvement over the standard uniform Dave was accustomed to seeing her in, Kayanne couldn't have scripted a more flattering reaction to her appearance. He stood on the stoop with appreciation glittering in his dark eyes. Seeing herself reflected in that admiring masculine gaze, she could almost believe herself to be Cinderella for the night.

Yet she didn't have any magic slippers to prevent Prince Charming from hearing some nasty comment about the wayward, raggedy wild child of her youth....

Suddenly sorry she'd ever asked him to accompany her tonight, Kayanne wondered how hard it would be to convince Dave to stop at the nearest bar and blow off all that nonsense she'd spouted earlier about making amends.

Before she had a chance to ask, her mother came up behind her and asked Dave in. Giving Kayanne a thumbs-up sign behind his back, Suzanne took his jacket and hung it up in the hallway closet.

"You're quite an improvement over the boys Kay usually brings home," she told him after proper introductions were made.

Kayanne winced.

"He's not a boy, Mom."

Dave didn't seem to mind. Smiling as he was directed to a well-worn chair with crocheted doilies on the arms and headrest, he appeared blissfully unaware of being led to an execution by firing squad—a barrage of questions instead of actual bullets.

Thrown by the use of her given name, Dave asked for clarification by repeating it. "Kay?"

"Kayanne is her stage name," her mother explained. "Of course, she can go by that in the big city where it's considered chic to change your name—and I suppose your principles as well—but back home, she'll always be my little girl, plain old Kay Anne Aldarmann."

Shuddering to hear her worst fears so blithely articulated, Kayanne pointed that out. "You make me sound like a stripper, Mom."

Blushing, Mrs. Aldarmann protested so vehemently that Dave took pity on her. "Not old—and definitely not plain," he interjected. "In fact, you look gorgeous tonight, Kayanne."

Relieved that he wasn't going to torment her with the name she'd deliberately abandoned, she rewarded him with a grateful smile. Her mother was right. Dave Evans wasn't at all like the men she usually dated.

He was far too nice.

Maybe Kayanne had simply been around vain male models competing with her for the limelight so long that she'd forgotten what it was like to be with someone who treated her as though she were something special. Unbidden, an image of her father flashed into her mind. It was a grainy mental picture of a big man with callused hands teaching his daughter to dance by letting her stand on the top of his worn work boots as he moved his feet in time to a country song on the radio.

"Someday my little princess will grow up to be the belle of the ball. I just hope I live long enough to see it," he'd told her over Hank Williams's lonesome lyrics.

Kayanne struggled against the lump in her throat that threatened to suffocate her.

Hoping to staunch the painful flow of memories with a quick exit, she announced, "We'd better get going."

Realizing that was typical of the way she handled her emotions, she wondered if her grown-up losses might not seem so unmanageable if she'd ever learned to truly mourn as a child instead of avoiding her feelings. Would she have ever learned to love herself if she'd been able to forgive her father for abandoning her?

As tempting as these insights were, Kayanne refused to think about that now. She grabbed her purse—a black beaded number just big enough to hold a tube of lipstick and tiny bottle of French perfume—and prepared to leave. Her ever obstinate mother, however, insisted on a modicum of polite conversation before being abandoned for the evening. She was nowhere near done grilling her prospective son-in-law on his background and future plans.

In the middle of her inquiries, Dave spied the Aldarmann Wall of Fame. Over her daughter's objections, Suzanne proceeded to point out what everyone else in town already knew.

"You mean you didn't know that Kay's famous?" she asked incredulously.

Dave gave her a funny, hurt look. "No," he replied. "That's a little something your daughter neglected to mention."

Kayanne tugged at his sleeve but couldn't budge him. With an eye to Sherlock Holmes, he examined the myriad prints lining the wall that chronicled her life from kindergarten to her first photo in a mail-order catalogue to the latest cover shot of a well-respected fashion magazine. His brown eyes widened in sudden recognition.

"I'll be damned," he exclaimed. "No wonder you look so familiar."

Having opened Pandora's box, Mrs. Aldarmann was finally content to let the two of them go on their way.

"Have fun tonight," she called from the front porch. "And don't worry about getting home at a reasonable hour on such a special night."

Kayanne rolled her eyes in the darkness as Dave escorted her to his vehicle. She was touched by his gentlemanly insistence on opening the door for her. With a thank you and a smile, she folded her long legs into his sporty Crossfire and settled into the butter-soft leather interior. Dave slid into the driver's seat and smoothly shifted into first gear.

"I had you figured for an SUV kind of guy," she told him.

"Left it home in the garage. I thought this suited you better."

A lot of things about him suited Kayanne better than she might have ever imagined. Nice car. Nice home. Nice guy. Dave Evans was definitely a change.

The expensive ring on his right hand was another indication that he was doing all right with his writing. Kayanne doubted he could afford his current standard of living on a teacher's wages alone. In the glare of a stoplight, she considered the possibility that he was just another joker up to his eyeballs in hock. In the city, she'd learned firsthand how thin the layer of glitz separating the rich from the homeless could be. Somehow Dave seemed more solid than the flashy wannabes who so often shadowed the rich and famous using any member of that elite group to advance their own status.

The truth was Kayanne wasn't sure how to act around a man—a gentleman—who wasn't out to use her. Yet one more thing destined to throw her off balance tonight.

Dave's sense of guilt compounded with every passing mile. The second Kayanne had met him at the door wearing that amazing dress, his writer's sense of objectivity had been shot all to hell. He'd agreed to accompany her not out of any saintly desire to do the right thing by her, but as a means of forwarding his novel. Of course, that wasn't to say that he didn't appreciate being seen with such a stunning woman in public.

And being alone with her later.

Just the thought of it made him grow hard. Glad that it was dark, Dave hoped he had enough time to get his hormones under control before reaching their destination.

Spice had an equally unsettling effect on him. Having supplanted the main character in his book, Kayanne's alter ego refused to come out to play when beckoned by his muse. Lately she'd been particularly obtuse, lounging around the pool naked, casually dropping the names of other lovers in an attempt to make him jealous. That the ploy was working had Dave questioning his own mental health.

He suspected that the only way he was going to find out who had murdered Jasmine was to explore the boundaries of Kayanne's real life. Her invitation to this class reunion couldn't have provided him with a more direct avenue to her past than had she offered herself up for voluntary hypnosis.

What Dave hadn't counted on was having any tender feelings toward her beyond the overwhelming sense of lust that she always evoked in him. It was far easier fantasizing about Kayanne as some kind of untouchable temptress or an incorrigible bad girl before meeting the straitlaced mother who apparently wanted nothing more than to see her daughter happy. He was touched by the fact that although she was clearly conflicted about her daughter's fame, Mrs. Aldarmann was also proud of Kayanne's accomplishments.

Who wouldn't be? Especially considering the humble upbringing.

Having seen Kayanne's face splashed all over the media for the past few years, Dave felt like a complete idiot not to have recognized her. He'd been intrigued by this mysterious woman's circumstances before, but now his curiosity spiked as high as his testosterone level— far beyond any measure of pure literary interest. The fact that "plain old Kay Anne Aldarmann" had grown up in such modest circumstances only made her that much more fascinating as a character. Dave suspected that whether she wanted to admit it or not, Kayanne had left a part of her heart in this rugged western town that she would have to reclaim before moving on with her life.

"Why didn't you tell me who you were?" he asked.

Although on one level, Dave considered himself a cad, mining this woman's life for his own creative needs, on another, he dismissed such qualms as being integral to the writing process. His job was to record his observations of real life before filtering them through a screen of fiction.

"I did," she insisted. "If you want to know why I didn't tell you about my modeling background, rest assured that it wasn't because I was afraid of intimidating you."

Dave wondered how she managed to turn this back on him and avoid any explanation in the process. He was on the verge of asking her why she was working at the Evening Star Manor, when she reached over and covered his hand on the gearshift.

"There's still plenty of time to change your mind about going to this thing."

Dave heard a note of hope in her voice and felt a tremble run through her. As silky as her voice, her touch almost sent him driving into the ditch. It was embarrassing. He hadn't felt so befuddled on a first date since he'd been a teenager. It wasn't just Kayanne's raw beauty that affected him so deeply, either.

"Are you kidding?" he replied. "What man doesn't dream of taking a supermodel to a high-school reunion? The only thing that could be better would be if it were *my* reunion."

As nerdy as he'd considered himself in high school, Dave liked to think of his old chums drooling as he sauntered into his alma mater with Kayanne on his arm. It struck him as odd that they had more in common than he'd ever imagined. Kayanne's upbringing in a trailer park might be far different from his privileged childhood in an upscale neighborhood, but the fact that she was still struggling against her mother's expectations had an all too familiar ring to it. He could no more imagine this wild creature cooped up in such an uninspired home than he could envision himself donning the heavy mantle of a family business that left him feeling tepid.

As pleasant as Mrs. Aldarmann had been to him, Dave sensed oppression in the stifling borders of her world. He could understand why Kayanne would be tempted to deny her roots and bolt the instant opportunity had presented itself. It was harder to figure out why she had returned. He suspected that whatever had brought her back was the same impulse that would someday turn his own steps home to sort out who he'd once been—and who he wanted to become.

Worried that Kayanne might make a run for it at the next stoplight, Dave forced his meandering thoughts back to her original query about whether he would rather be someplace else.

"Have you changed *your* mind about going to this thing?" he asked.

There were lots of places they could go instead, and it didn't have to be to a bar. Kayanne's previous references to making amends hadn't been lost on him. He wanted no part of pushing someone who might be struggling with addiction off the wagon.

"No," she said with all the enthusiasm of someone about to undergo a pelvic exam. "This is something I need to do. Probably should have done a long time ago. But I have to warn you. You might hear some ugly things about me tonight. And most of them are probably true...."

Seven

Kayanne used a minimum of words to guide Dave to the high school. As tempted as she was to ask him to avoid driving by Pete Nargas's old house, it was along the most direct route, and there was little point in postponing the onslaught of feelings that the reunion itself was sure to evoke. Unable to avert her gaze, she felt a stab of guilt as they passed by the Nargas home. The place seemed downcast, as though the vitality had seeped out. The old porch swing needed a fresh coat of paint.

The sight stirred memories of holding hands, wishing upon falling stars and stealing kisses under Pete's little brothers' and sisters' ever-vigilant surveillance. Kayanne smiled at the thought of his father flipping the porch light off and on three times in quick succession to let them know it was time to call it a night before their innocent kisses could get out of hand. Through the open car window she caught a whiff of fragrant honeysuckle. In her absence, the bush had almost taken over Pete's bedroom window. As sweet as those blossoms, Kayanne had yet to find anything as redolent as her first love.

She missed the stability of Pete's loving family almost as much as she missed him. Kayanne wished there was some way of opening the lines of communication between them. But she couldn't. Not without hurting them in the process. Even Beth cautioned her about making amends if it caused the other person undue pain.

As Kayanne and Dave pulled into the parking lot, she felt her heartbeat race. It went into warp speed when Dave opened the double doors of the gymnasium and she stepped back into the past in which she'd been another person. A professional who'd endured the perils of a career that spanned both coasts, Kayanne managed a dazzling smile as she swept into the room. The distinctive odor of that gym instantly took her to her sophomore year when she'd failed to make the cheerleading squad. All arms and legs with a mouthful of braces, she'd lacked the self-confidence, not to mention the coordination, to pull off a winning routine.

Who could have predicted gawky Kay Anne Aldarmann would emerge from the painfully awkward cocoon of adolescence as such a beautiful butterfly? Certainly not her. She still found it ironic that women all over the world attempted to duplicate the auburn mane that had once been the bane of her childhood.

Even now she wondered why she felt compelled to prove herself to this particular group of peers after she'd already proven herself to the entire world.

Drawing on her runway experience, she calmed the butterflies in her stomach as she filled out her name tag with an artistic flourish.

Kayanne

Just one word. The name she'd picked for herself when she'd turned away from this town. Her last name was as unnecessary as the required tag she dutifully pinned on her chest. Recognition caused a stir as everybody paused to stare. Operating as if that stir didn't exist at all, Kayanne took Dave's hand and allowed him to escort her across the gym floor. His hand felt strong, sinewy, hairy and every bit as masculine and reassuring as its owner. Suddenly there was warmth deep inside Kayanne where before only a cold, stinging wind had howled.

The two of them made a striking pair. Kayanne looked as though she'd stepped off the cover of a fashion magazine, and Dave was a dream in a pair of dark slacks and a silk dress shirt. A diamond tie tack glinted in the dim lights. His all-American good looks rivaled those of any of the pretty boys who'd accompanied her on prestigious shoots around the world. As the most eligible bachelor in town, his presence by her side proved far more shocking than any rebel Kayanne's old classmates might have expected to accompany her. She gave him her best superstar smile.

"Lots of eligible single women here," she pointed

out. "Here's your chance to introduce yourself to the local lovelies."

"Why bother when I'm with the most beautiful woman in the room?"

It was such a sweet thing to say that Kayanne almost stopped in mid-stride to kiss him. Covertly scanning the crowd, she thought the better of it though. Why reward him by risking his sterling reputation? Not when he was doing her a huge favor just by being here.

Looking around, Kayanne was surprised by her old classmates' appearances. Prepared to be shocked by the passage of time, she discovered it wasn't going to be as hard as she'd imagined matching the adolescent faces she remembered with the countenances that were regarding her so cautiously. The head cheerleader was just as cute as Kayanne remembered, and though the quarterback was sporting a little gray at the temples, he still looked hot. A few schoolmates had widening girths and balding pates, but overall everybody looked pretty good.

The fact that people were already gravitating to the same old cliques they'd hung with then only intensified Kayanne's growing sense of panic. It seemed little had changed in the ten years she'd been gone. Before the night was over she worried that the same old people would be saying the same old things about her.

Banners hanging from the ceiling attested to the mighty Broncs' state and regional championships. Faded felt had stood the test of time better than the athletes who'd earned those titles, many of whom had long ago passed from this world. As Dave steered her across the gym floor toward the punch bowl, Kayanne felt the whispers at her back as keenly as pinpricks. She hadn't felt this self-conscious since the fateful night of her senior prom when she'd broken up with Pete Nargas and had changed the course of both their lives forever. That was the last time she remembered dating a genuinely nice guy—until letting Dave into her life.

Was it Pete's ghost murmuring his name in her ear? Or merely another classmate, with a long memory and the need to blame her for Pete's decision, who was reviving old, hurtful rumors?

Kayanne asked Dave to get her a glass of punch from the nonalcoholic bowl. She appreciated the fact that he did so without comment. Having been the girl who'd spiked the punch at more than one school dance, she knew the irony would be lost on many of her classmates. She couldn't count the number of people she knew who had literally spent a fortune on some expensive treatment center only to fall back into deadly habits the minute they rejoined their usual crowd of friends. So it was that sobriety was a salty dish that Kayanne dared not ask anyone to share with her.

Glad to have something to occupy her hands, she sipped slowly, hoping to make this drink last a good long while. Suddenly a tiny woman with steel-gray hair cut into the shape of a helmet zeroed in on them from across the floor. Kayanne's face broke into a wide smile. She asked Dave to hold her cup before opening her arms to her former mentor.

"Mrs. Rawlins!"

"I'm so glad you could make it," the woman said, wrapping herself around Kayanne's waist and giving it a good squeeze.

Kayanne couldn't remember being so glad to see a familiar, welcoming face.

"I heard they're giving you an award tonight," she said. "I wouldn't miss that for the world."

"The award is inconsequential to your being here," Mrs. Rawlins assured her. "I'm retiring this year, and I suspect this is the administration's way of making sure I follow through on that promise."

Kayanne laughed. "I can't imagine SHS without you. The school just won't be the same," she said, meaning it.

Had it not been for the likes of the indomitable Gertrude Rawlins, Kayanne probably would have dropped out of school altogether.

"You look wonderful," Mrs. Rawlins said, stepping back to take a good look. "Even better than in print."

"I hope you don't subscribe to any of those awful tabloids that go out of their way to make people look their worst," Kayanne said with chagrin. "I have to admit that I'm feeling somewhat ancient tonight. You, on the other hand, don't look a day older than when I left."

Mrs. Rawlins clucked in disbelief. She turned to Dave. "If you wouldn't begrudge an old lady a few minutes, I'd like to show Kayanne off to my colleagues, some of whom were so foolish as to actually question whether she'd make it big."

"Or even graduate," Kayanne admitted in all honesty. Recalling the unpleasantness associated with her senior year, she added, "I suspect you're the only teacher who remembers me fondly."

"Don't be ridiculous," Mrs. Rawlins said brusquely. "I distinctly remember you having the intelligence and courage to match your looks. I hope you're not still blaming yourself for what happened to Pete Nargas."

Dave's ears perked up. In truth his curiosity had little to do with developing the characters in his novel. He wondered if this Pete fellow was someone Kayanne had once loved. Someone she'd never gotten over? Did he have something to do with her fear of intimacy? Or the reason she'd left town so long ago?

"I'll wait for you here," Dave said, taking an observer's position against the nearest wall and making mental notes.

Festooned in the school colors of blue and gold, the scene took him back to his own high-school days. Crepe paper and handmade signs harkened to a less complicated time in his life. His adolescence hadn't been marked by the obvious hardships of Kayanne's; there had always been plenty of money in the Evans household. But growing up is never without pain. His family's expectations of him appeared to be the polar opposite of those with which Kayanne had been raised. If people seemed to expect failure from her, success was presumed for him. It wore the same starched and stiff shirt his father and grandfather had passed from one generation to the next. As tacky as Mrs. Aldarmann's Wall of Fame might seem, Dave wished that his parents were as supportive of his literary and academic successes as

Kayanne's mother was of her daughter's accomplishments, no matter how far removed they might be from her own pedantic life.

"You're an unusual specimen of wallflower," a sultry voice informed him.

It belonged to a blonde whose name tag identified her as Valerie Davis-Mills. Dave wondered whether her reed-thin figure could be attributed to excessive dieting and compulsive exercising or just good genes. And he noticed that she wasn't wearing a wedding ring.

"Didn't I see you walk in with Kay Anne?" she asked.

"I don't know. Did you?"

Her laugh was a throaty gurgle. The next thing Dave knew, she'd stepped closer and proceeded to launch into a line of questioning that made him feel decidedly uncomfortable.

"You're not from around here, are you?" Valerie guessed with a knowing smile.

Since the question was rhetorical, she didn't wait for his response before asking another. "How long have you known our little homegrown celebrity?"

"Not long."

"I don't suppose Kay's ever mentioned Pete Nargas to you?"

"No, but I can't say this is the first time I've heard the name."

Torn between his curiosity and loyalty to Kayanne, Dave tried to remain polite while keeping his answers short and noncommittal.

"I wouldn't think so." Valerie nodded meaningfully.

She looked disappointed when Dave didn't follow up by asking her to share any of her secrets.

"What about a Jason DeWinter?"

Assuming Jason and Pete were old boyfriends, Dave felt a sudden need to put an end to a conversation that led him to believe Valerie was the type of person who relied on innuendo to make herself feel better. It had the opposite effect on him. There were better ways to research a fictional character than by engaging in shameless gossip. He shook his head.

"I'm afraid not. The truth is I'm a whole lot more interested in the woman Kayanne is now than the girl she was back in high school."

Although Valerie's voice remained saccharine, her smile turned brittle.

"How very sweet of you," she crooned, reaching up to pat his shoulder. Her eyebrows shot up when she discovered the muscles beneath that shirt. "By the way, what is it that *you* do, Mr…?"

"Evans. Dave Evans. I'm presently unemployed but will be teaching English at the college this fall. With an emphasis on creative writing."

Valerie looked positively enthralled. "Right here? In little old Sheridan? You know, I've thought about taking a writing class myself. I have a stack of poems that I'd just love to have you help me dust off…."

When she finally left him to join a nearby group of old friends, Dave didn't have to strain to hear what she had to report over the patter of a DJ who was cranking out nostalgic tunes of the 1990s. Dave tapped his foot in time to the music. Everyone in his parents' social circle enrolled their children in formal as well as popular dance lessons. As much as he'd hated it at the time, as an adult he was glad not to have to worry about crushing his date's instep with his size-twelve shoes.

"You don't think she's actually got the nerve to approach Jason DeWinter in public, do you?" he heard a shocked voice ask Valerie.

Dave felt disgusted. If he'd come here looking for dirt, those *ladies* were unloading it by the dump load in the middle of the floor. It was hard to believe that anything so petty could stir a sense of jealousy in him, but it did. He didn't even know the much maligned Mr. DeWinter, but suddenly Dave wanted to punch his lights out.

He'd always assumed that high school was hell for homely girls. It had never occurred to him that it might be less than heavenly for beautiful girls as well. No wonder Kayanne hadn't wanted to come to this reunion alone. No wonder she'd thought about having a drink to steady her nerves. He could use one himself.

He pushed off from the wall and sauntered over to where Mrs. Rawlins was reintroducing Kayanne to her colleagues. Slipping an arm possessively around her waist, he felt her tremble. It was the only hint of nervousness to be discerned from a woman who carried herself as coolly as a queen. Dave's chest grew tight as unfamiliar feelings swelled up inside of him.

The writer's objectivity he'd always clung to dissipated beneath the warmth of the look Kayanne gave him. Until now he had never seen the slightest glimmer of weakness in those mystical eyes of hers. It utterly destroyed all of the signs he'd posted around his heart to keep trespassers out.

Dave wasn't quite sure exactly what he was protecting this woman from. He only knew that it was imperative that he be by her side for the rest of the evening and that he treat her like a precious object in the face of mudslinging and outright envy. That wasn't particularly difficult to do. None of the men in the room could take their eyes off her, and Dave was no exception. On one hand, he felt like the luckiest guy in the world to have earned this woman's trust. And on the other, like the biggest schmuck on the face of the earth for secretly betraying her.

As Mrs. Rawlins left them to take a place of honor at the table set up in the front of the room, Dave wondered if it would ever occur to Kayanne that she had far less to fear from the specters of her past than she did from him. If she ever were to read his manuscript and put two and two together, she would undoubtedly be hurt by some of the jagged descriptions he'd written. Likely she would be offended by the lustful turn his plot had taken.

Kayanne dragged him into the present moment by squeezing his hand hard.

"Whatever happens in the next few minutes," she whispered, "promise that you won't leave me."

Dave's muscles tensed as he followed her gaze to a man in his late forties. Somewhat short and slight of stature, he still retained a handsome visage with his bright blue eyes. The fact that he wasn't wearing a name tag on his brown tweed jacket indicated to Dave that he was probably a member of the faculty. The man suddenly grew red in the face as he recognized Kayanne. Had she not stuck out her hand and forced him to acknowledge her, Dave suspected the fellow would have bolted for the door.

"Mr. DeWinter," she said. "What a surprise to see you again."

Eight

Kayanne studied the man quivering in front of her with something akin to shock. In high school, through the eyes of innocence, she'd viewed Jason DeWinter as the wisest and handsomest man alive—almost a kind of god. Later, in drunken contemplation of the wrongs done to her, she'd convinced herself that he was nothing short of a monster—a married adult who had deliberately manipulated a young girl's grief for his own gain. A sexual predator of the worst sort.

A wolf in trusted counselor's clothing.

She was having trouble getting her mind around the fact that this man with the limp, sweaty handshake wasn't an imposter. Neither deity nor devil, Jason was as mortal as she herself was. And it occurred to her for the first time in her life that he might even be more vulnerable.

It would be a lie to say that Kayanne hadn't wavered between wanting to make amends for any part she may have played in causing him to stray from the path of marital fidelity and dressing him down in front of the entire throng for a fraud and a sexual deviant. Out of the corner of her eye, she noticed Dave's hands curled into fists where they hung at his sides. She took comfort in the fact that he was willing to rush to her defense without even knowing the history leading to this confrontation. It was tempting simply to turn tail before he could hear the sordid details of her misspent youth, but Kayanne felt it important that Dave know her for who she was—and what the community saw her as. If he wanted to deepen their relationship after that, Kayanne would know she'd found something special.

Something worth sticking around for.

"Kay? Kay Anne Aldarmann?" Jason asked, looking as if he were unable to believe his eyes.

His ability to speak appeared as impaired as his vision.

"I didn't…realize you'd be here…. You look…terrific…."

Kayanne bit down on her tongue to keep from commenting on *his* appearance.

And you look so very small and old and frightened that it's hard not to feel sorry for you.

Jason cleared his throat. "I understand that you've done…quite well for yourself…. I'm happy for you, Kay. Really…I am."

She had to fight the urge to look away from the man who had caused her such heartache. Having come this far, however, she saw no reason to dance around the issue any longer.

"I don't know exactly how well I'm doing," she replied. "I'm back living at home, working at a menial job and trying to get my head screwed on straight after all these years."

Her old high-school counselor swallowed hard. Looking around to see how many pairs of eyes were watching him, he moved closer, presumably so it would be harder to eavesdrop. When Dave took a menacing step in his direction, he retreated accordingly.

"I'm sorry," Jason said.

His voice cracked. His eyes watered. And Kayanne realized with a start that he truly meant it. His unexpected remorse was balm to old wounds that had never properly healed. She wondered if he had been carrying around his own fair share of guilt for the past decade. In all the times she'd run through this particular scenario in her head, she had never once imagined feeling pity for the man who had abused his position and taken advantage of a confused teenage girl.

Tonight, however, time, distance and sobriety altered her perspective. Instead of humiliating him by slapping him across the face or curling up in a fetal ball and letting him hurt her for another decade, Kayanne felt an amazing change come over her. It was as if she were watching herself from a distance and wondering why she had ever given such a scared little pip-squeak so much power. How much of her life had she wasted holding the past against the future? Weary of carrying around the heavy burden of resentment, she asked herself what good could possibly come of nursing her bitterness any longer.

"I forgive you," she said, feeling surprised to hear those words come out of her mouth.

Suddenly a strange, tingling sensation shot from her fingertips throughout her whole body as a brilliant light enveloped her. She felt warm all over—weightless and free. Jason continued talking as if completely unaware of the light surrounding them. Looking to Dave for support, Kayanne found him equally unaffected by what she'd once heard called a white-light experience. Dave was glowering at Jason as if considering the pleasure of tearing him limb from limb as the other man tried ineffectually to explain himself in a rush of words.

Kayanne wondered if she was going crazy.

"That was such an unhappy time for both of us," Jason was saying. "You were dealing with Pete's tragic decision and you came to my office shortly afterwards blaming yourself. You were so beautiful, my wife and I were having marital trouble, and I was young and stupid. I was also worried that you might try something like Pete did."

So you slept with me, a high-school senior who wasn't nearly as sexually experienced as she would have everyone believe?

Kayanne cut him off. The power of forgiveness was too extraordinary to risk under the weight of misspoken words.

"There's no reason to go into it all over again. People make mistakes," she said simply.

Standing here all these years later, she was able finally to grasp the truth. The man she had trusted above all others hadn't intentionally hurt her. In her hour of need, she'd turned to an egotistical, inexperienced counselor for help and mistaken what he'd had to offer for love. Embroiled in his own problems and caught up in trying to comfort her, Jason had discovered an attraction over which he'd had little control. That didn't mean he hadn't exercised poor judgment and that his decisions hadn't hurt her deeply when the community had rallied behind him to cast her as the Jezebel who'd killed their favorite son and had made a married man forsake his vows. It just meant that Kayanne was ready to let go of that painful part of her past and move on. At long last.

"I wish my wife had been able to see things that way. She filed for divorce shortly after you left," Jason said, blinking back tears.

"I'm sorry."

Kayanne really was. More for his wife than for him. It couldn't have been easy for her living under a cloud of doubt and rumor. And it must have also been hard competing with all the needy young girls who put her husband on a pedestal far above the geeky adolescent boys their own age.

Jason wet his lips. "I don't suppose there's any chance that you and I could possibly get together for some—"

This time it was Dave who cut him off.

"No," he said, leaning in so far that the other man had

to take a step backward or risk falling over. "She most certainly can't. Not ever. Not with you."

As much as Kayanne resented having anybody speak for her in such a manner, she couldn't help but be touched by such a gallant, protective move. The fact that Dave had been privy to one of the most revealing and unflattering conversations of her life should by all rights have sent him scurrying for the door. That he was still there by her side ready to do battle for the sake of her tattered reputation was incredibly moving.

If she wasn't careful, she might just fall in love with such a hopelessly romantic fool. And that could only spell *Disaster* with a capital *D* for them both.

Dave raised his closed fist from where he had it cocked at his side to emphasize his point. Kayanne put a hand gently on his arm to restrain him.

"That's not such a good idea."

Although neither man was sure if she was addressing him or the other, Kayanne defused the situation with a soft look.

"Would you mind dancing with me now?" she asked Dave.

Without so much as another word, he took her in his arms and swung her onto the dance floor, casting a final dark look over his shoulder at the infamous Mr. DeWinter.

That sorry son of a bitch!

Dave didn't claim to understand all of what had just happened. Only enough to be enraged at the idea of a grown man abusing the trust of his position with a minor.

Why Kayanne had taken the brunt of this town's ill will as a teenager while DeWinter was still a school counselor was beyond Dave. At the very least, the creep should have been fired. Running him out of town on a rail would have been more to Dave's liking. The man's audacity sickened him. You would think the little pervert would have been worried about Kayanne's father killing him.

Then he remembered. Kayanne had had no father or burly brothers to protect her. The thought of her fending for herself at such a young age caused him to pull her even tighter against his chest. He was glad that the slow song the DJ played lent itself to intimacy. Kayanne felt so good in his arms that it seemed as if she had been special ordered to fit against the hard planes of his body. Strong both physically and emotionally, she didn't fit the stereotypical anorexic, self-absorbed waif so often associated with supermodels. Yet it was her unexpected vulnerability that caused Dave to wrap himself around her in an effort to protect her from those who seemed to take delight in her troubles.

He couldn't believe she'd actually been able to forgive that little slimeball. It wasn't something Spice would do—and yet another indication that he had sorely misjudged her real-life inspiration. Beneath Kayanne's initial brashness was a woman of greater depth and character than he'd ever imagined.

And beneath the fabric of her slinky dress was a body he couldn't get out of his mind no matter how hard he tried. During waking or sleeping hours.

Dave's desire to make the lecherous Mr. DeWinter

swallow his teeth like a handful of Chiclets gave way to the overwhelming desire for something more carnal. Beneath a twirling mirrored ball, he fell headlong into Kayanne's warm gaze. As green as the first blades of a springtime meadow, her eyes had the power to melt all his defenses.

"I can't believe how good you are to me," she whispered into his ear.

Smelling like heaven, Kayanne leaned in even closer to make sure Dave heard that ridiculous assertion. With the evidence of his arousal pressed hot against her, he dared not allow her to pull away for fear that everyone else in the room would be aware of his lack of self-control as well. Holding her against him, he swore softly in response to her assessment of his character. The way Kayanne was looking at him as though he were some kind of knight in shining armor made him feel a sham.

How could he possibly tell her that his armor was tarnished by the fact that he'd agreed to escort her tonight for the sake of getting into her head? And that he was similarly motivated to get into her pants? When she laid her head trustingly against his shoulder, Dave resolved to keep her safe from all men—himself included.

"I think you're amazing," he told her.

"Thank you," she said, tilting her head up to look straight into his eyes and hold his soul up to examination. "For being there for me."

Something hard stuck sideways in Dave's throat. He couldn't imagine that Kayanne could have ever brought herself to confide any of the details of her involvement with Mr. DeWinter in her morally upright mother. Nor could he imagine her being able to keep her mother from hearing embellished versions from interested friends and neighbors. In a community that prided itself on everyone knowing everything about everybody, it would have been impossible to keep such a secret.

Dave wondered if Kayanne had run off to the big city to avoid facing her mother's disappointment. Or just to make life easier for Jason DeWinter.

The unshed tears glistening in her eyes made Dave want to rise above his own selfish desires and become what she foolishly believed him to be. A white-hatted hero. What did it matter that they were as ill-suited as Don Quixote and his beloved Dulcinea?

Never had Dave had such intense feelings for a woman. Stroking her hair, he reveled in its texture and felt Kayanne soften in his arms. He wondered how long he could continue holding her up with his own boneless limbs.

Her breath was as sweet against his skin as the fragrance she wore. Dave had been dreaming of Kayanne's kisses ever since Rose had so rudely interrupted their first one.

Brushing his lips gently across hers, he heard a murmur of protest die in her throat. His fingers tangled in her hair.

He touched her lower lip with the tip of his tongue, inviting her full participation. Warm and soft and inviting, her mouth opened expectantly. He felt her tremble in his arms. And heard a moan that echoed his own.

The music, the people, the surrounding scenery all faded into nothingness. Blinded to everything but the feel and taste and perfection of this woman, he sealed them together in a fusion of heat and longing.

To embrace fire without self-immolating was something new to a man who, if he were honest with himself, was more than a little intimidated by Kayanne's wild side—and notorious past. Like many of his colleagues, he sometimes found it difficult to live beyond the pages of his books. And this desire was nothing like he'd ever written before.

He kissed her long and deep and hard. She kissed him back, holding onto his shoulders, digging in with her nails in a way that brought more pleasure than pain.

"What do you say we get out of here," Kayanne suggested in a whisper that was full of promise.

As chance would have it, at that exact moment, a drunk collided with them, bringing the rest of the world back into sharp focus. In spite of the fact that he'd spilled his drink all over Kayanne's designer dress, the bleary-eyed man stepped back and assumed the posture of someone *expecting* an apology.

"Hey," he slurred, concentrating on Kayanne's name badge as if it were fading in and out of focus.

He took a hiccup step in her direction and squinted at her. When recognition finally dawned on him, he blew enough alcohol in her face to make her draw back in disgust.

"Hey, buddy," he said, poking a finger in Dave's chest. "You'd better be careful. The black widow kills her prey after she mates."

Gentle by nature, Dave didn't know what exactly came

over him as he stood looking down on the man's prone body less than a minute later. His hand hurt where it had scraped against the man's belt buckle. He couldn't quite believe that he'd actually hit that jackass, but the evidence lay irrefutably whimpering on the floor in front of him. Usually drunks didn't have this kind of an effect on him. Tired of all the innuendos, snide remarks and flat-out maliciousness directed at Kayanne over the evening, Dave had struck back the only way he knew how.

The hurt expression on her face had unleashed a beast in him. As much as Dave hated to admit it, he felt little remorse about driving his fist into the bum's soft belly and leaving him crumpled in a heap. When the screams around them died down, he donned his best Cary Grant imitation of a good-natured man pushed past his limit. Regarding the assembled crowd staring at him in appalled curiosity, he put forth a question to all of them.

"Does anyone else have anything nasty to say about my date?"

Nine

Seeing how it was a rhetorical question, Kayanne didn't wait around for an answer to Dave's inquiry. They remained only long enough to see the drunk on the floor get dragged away by some of his friends and to listen to Mrs. Rawlins's short speech before making a quiet getaway.

Once outside and safely tucked into Dave's car, Kayanne wasn't sure how she was supposed to feel. Angry that he felt the need to protect her when she was perfectly capable of doing that for herself—as she had been doing for the past ten years? Embarrassed to have been made a spectacle of in front of her old mentor and classmates? Or grateful that a knight in shining armor had stepped forward to defend her questionable honor?

Mostly Kayanne was confused. Forgiving the man whom she'd been blaming her troubles on for the past decade left a hole in her life she needed to fill with something other than contempt. With the exception of a few notable jerks and one mouthy lush, most of her old classmates had actually been quite warm and complimentary. And the man whom she'd initially seen as the most unlikely romantic interest in her future—her date for the evening—was melting the polar ice field of her heart faster than a Popsicle in a microwave.

Life was proving far more unpredictable than Kayanne could have ever imagined. Her world was spinning out of control. It felt rather like being drunk. Alcohol chipped away at inhibitions, letting her take chances that she would never make when sober then providing her with a handy excuse for her behavior the next day. Tonight Kayanne was on the verge of taking the biggest risk in her life with her eyes wide open and her senses unimpaired.

Could there be anything more frightening than falling in love stone-cold sober?

Her standard approach to dating was to use men before they could use her first. It was a strategy borne out of a painful string of doomed relationships intended to satisfy the libido without engaging the heart. Experience whispered in her ear to take things slowly. She refused to listen.

Dave and she were both grown-ups who understood the score. They were consenting adults who, for whatever reason, needed to carry this relationship to the next level. What difference did it make that such a step might be their final one? After becoming intimate, Kayanne couldn't imagine resuming their friendship as it had once been and waving cordially to one another on the street as if nothing had passed between them.

Dave pulled up in front of his house. He leaned forward and put one hand on the side of her headrest. With the other, he tucked a lock of hair behind her ear. The gentleness of that small gesture sucked the breath out of her lungs.

"Would you like to come inside?" he asked her.

Finding her throat too tight to allow words out, Kayanne simply answered with a nod. No shy virgin, she felt out of sorts with herself for being so nervous. She had been with men before. Innumerable men had sought her out as an elixir for eternal youth. Or a status symbol that put them in an exclusive club of men who had slept with a supermodel. Kayanne herself had considered sex as a weapon ever since Pete Nargas had taught her the foolishness of love in its purest form.

What she was feeling for Dave was different from anything she'd ever felt before. Neither innocent nor manipulative, it was lust refined with genuine affection. And it was every bit as risky as that first sip of whiskey. Kayanne's sobriety was based on control, and since what she was feeling at the moment was far out of her control, she had to ask herself if it was possible to date casually and stay sober.

There was certainly nothing casual about the way her heart beat so wildly against her chest. Nor the roar in her ears caused by the blood thrumming through her veins. Later, she wouldn't be able to recall Dave opening the car door for her. Or the front door to his house. Or the door to his bedroom for that matter. He didn't carry her like some naive bride up the walk and over the threshold, but Kayanne couldn't remember her feet ever touching the ground either.

The rest of the evening, however, was indelibly etched into her memory.

Dave didn't wait to reach the bedroom before making his intentions crystal clear. He didn't bother asking her if she wanted a cup of coffee or needed to recap the events of the evening. Instead, he simply put his hands around her waist and pulled her to him. It was an act that could have easily been designed to show her just how much bigger and stronger he was than her. Instead it made Kayanne feel incredibly safe. There was no way this man would hurt her. Not physically.

Not intentionally.

Wrapping one arm around her waist, Dave stroked the bare skin of her exposed back with the other, deliberately grazing the sides of her breasts along the way. He was driving her crazy. Involuntarily, Kayanne arched like a cat and heard herself purr. She felt him reach for the delicate clasp at her neck, which he undid with an expert flick of his finger.

The silky fabric slipped away to reveal her bare breasts, and Kayanne fought the urge to cover herself. Her nipples tightened into perfect tight rosebuds as Dave stepped back to admire his handiwork.

"Wow," was all he could manage to say before following his gaze with greedy fingers. He touched her gently, cupping her in his big masculine hands, fondling her and brushing his palms across her taut nipples. Then he kneeled in front of her to take her in his mouth. He sucked with all of his mouth, teeth, lips and tongue all working together to render her powerless.

When her knees almost buckled and Kayanne could handle no more, she said in a raspy whisper, "Stand up."

When he complied, she rewarded him by grabbing both sides of his shirt and yanking it open. Buttons plinked as they hit the hardwood floor. She reached around to undo her own zipper. Her dress pooled on the floor. Dave pulled his shirt out of his pants, tore it off and draped it on the banister. Socks and shoes were abandoned on the way up the stairs. His briefs hung on the doorknob of his bedroom door.

Kayanne didn't take the time to appreciate the simple masculinity of Dave's bedroom with its sparsely decorated walls and big, comfy bed. One minute she was standing wearing nothing but lacy panties with a matching garter belt holding up her nylons, and the next she was lying naked on her back atop the fluffy comforter. They didn't bother turning the sheets back.

They were two people coming apart at the seams, desperate to find out whether kisses that melted bodies could do the same to their souls. Under the circumstances, it was a wonder that Dave had the wherewithal to remember the condoms he kept in the top drawer of his dresser. A tangle of limbs, they clawed at one another in a frenzy. Naked flesh was hot upon naked flesh.

Searing, slick, demanding, the feelings simmering between them since the first time they'd exchanged curious glances came to the surface as immediate and scalding as lava pumping over the edge of a volcano.

Entwining her hands at the nape of Dave's neck, Kayanne riffled through his hair and found it soft to the touch. She breathed in the musky fragrance that was only part cologne and all him. It stimulated her need to taste him. She licked the salt from his neck and found it good upon her tongue.

His hands clasped the back of her head and drew her away so that she had no choice but to look straight into the eyes of the man who was about to make love to her.

"Hurry," she commanded.

Willing and wanting, she had never been so ready for a man.

Happy to comply, Dave positioned himself strategically over her. Women could say what they would about size not mattering, but Kayanne begged to differ. When Dave showed himself to her in all his masculine splendor, she gasped. Then ran a painted fingernail down the length of his hard sex. And up again.

His skin stretched even tighter. She took him in one hand and squeezed gently, lingering when he moaned. Holding him thus, she felt the full extent of her feminine power.

"You like holding me in the palm of your hand, don't you?" he asked, and she knew he meant it as much symbolically as literally. The hard edge to his voice told Kayanne that she was playing with fire.

"I do," she admitted, succumbing to her need to have him inside her.

Dave paused only long enough to reach for the ripe globes of her breasts. He held them in his hands as if they were matching chalices of pure gold, then dipped his head to suck greedily at their swollen nipples. Kayanne fought the urge to beg him to take her immediately. He sheathed himself with protection before pressing himself against her engorged entrance and kissing her deeply. Unable to stand the sheer bliss of his lips and hands and manhood upon her at once, she tore her mouth away from his and screamed when he entered her.

Slick and hard, he filled her in ways that no other man ever had. Her scream echoed his moans of ecstasy. Grasping her buttocks in both hands, he plunged into her with an unnecessary apology on his lips.

"I don't want to hurt you," he murmured.

"You won't," she assured him, alternately mewling and purring.

I'll never let anybody hurt me again. Not even you....

Releasing his hold on her thick mane of hair, Dave pillaged her body with his hands. As a starving man savoring the rarest delicacy, he devoured her as if fearing nothing would ever taste as sweet again.

Kayanne couldn't make out the words he muttered. Were they words of love? Or oaths protesting her power over him?

Straining for release, he climaxed in an act that was poetry to behold. Usually Kayanne held herself back and watched with a certain amount of disinterest men's foolish attempts to dominate her either physically or emotionally. This time was different.

This time, Dave took her along with him for the ride, cresting only when he was certain she was ready to climax. It happened so fast that she had no chance to restrain herself, to pull back emotionally, let alone to analyze the situation. Never had Kayanne made love with such abandon. Never had she felt so free. So wild. So completely beautiful inside and out.

When Dave exploded in her arms, it was all she could do to keep from crying.

Holding on to her last shard of dignity, she dug her nails into his broad back and smothered any endearments that might make her sound needy. It was a long trip back to the reality of her own skin. If there was such a thing as heaven on earth, Kayanne was convinced that this had to be it. It was as close to perfection as she had ever known.

And just as she'd feared, it was more addictive than any spirits she'd ever tried.

Slick and wet and spent, they clung to one another in the darkness as orphans tossed upon tumultuous emotional seas. The rare man who understood the value of after-play, Dave held her tenderly, stroking the length of her arm with his fingertips. His deep breath warmed her bare skin. Placing her head against his chest, Kayanne was reassured by the steady thumping of his heart. She feathered kisses on his chest and contemplated the pull between the ordinary and the sublime. It was so powerful, it rivaled the miracle of the white light that had appeared out of nowhere to mend her tattered heart.

Was it possible that God was not stingy with His miracles as to grant but one a customer?

For a brief, shining moment, Kayanne let herself imagine someone as good and decent as Dave loving someone as tarnished and world-weary as herself. Images flashed into her mind's eye, imprinting themselves upon her soul. Wholesome images that were far from glamorous. And far more appealing. Images of Dave lifting her hair off her neck to nibble playfully while she did the dishes. Slapping his hand in jest as he sneaked a bite from the meal she had simmering on the stove. Waking him in the morning with a hot cup of coffee and a smattering of kisses. Cheerful morning glories entwined in the front picket fence. A baby curled up in a crib.

Of course, planting emotional roots meant taking risks, and Kayanne wasn't sure she could ever commit to that. Still, the possibility of starting life over with a man whose love went more than skin deep took hold of her imagination. And refused to let go.

Out of the darkness came a startling question that shattered their companionable silence along with any illusions Kayanne might have had about finding protection from the past in the sanctuary of Dave's strong arms.

"Would you mind telling me who Pete Nargas is?"

Kayanne wondered if he was asking because of that stupid "black widow" remark made at the reunion. As idiotic and irrational as the man who'd made it, the comment still had the power to wound her deeply.

"He was my first real boyfriend," she said, keeping her voice deliberately flat.

Dave drew a heart on her shoulder with his index finger. Kayanne had no idea why that tender gesture opened a door that had been nailed shut for so long, but suddenly she felt the need to share with him everything that she'd kept bottled up inside her.

"He was the hometown darling. Captain of the basketball team. Honor student. A genuinely nice boy."

The problem, she went on to explain, was that he fell madly in love with her.

"I, on the other hand, was more in love with the idea of being in love," she admitted. "But I did care for him a great deal. It was just that I had my own dreams at the time, and they didn't include enrolling in the local community college and being pregnant at seventeen."

She wondered why she should expect Dave to understand when no one else had. Did she sound as selfish to him as she sounded to herself?

And as guilty?

"Pete was obsessed with me. He couldn't handle it when I wanted to break up with him. Eventually, to spare his feelings, I accepted a promise ring that I shouldn't have and tried to make something work that wasn't meant to be. I finally broke up with him officially after the prom. It was an ugly scene. He threatened to kill me. When that failed to change my mind, he said he'd maim me so that no other man would ever want me. The thought of me being with anyone else drove him crazy, I guess."

The terror of his threats remained with her to this day. And were part of the reason she was afraid to let anyone get close to her.

It was hard not to interpret the silence that followed her disclosure as a personal indictment. Jagged blades of regret filled the space between them. Kayanne had never been able to forgive herself for what had happened next. She wished there was some way to make the re-telling easier.

There wasn't.

Kayanne hadn't spoken of the incident indepth to anyone except Jason DeWinter. Considering where that had gotten her, she was understandably hesitant to unlock that door again. Sighing, she wiped imaginary blood from her hands onto the sheet.

"He killed himself shortly after I broke up with him. Left a suicide note that everyone in town saw as a condemnation of me personally."

She took a moment to compose herself before continuing.

"Aside from the craziness at the end, Pete was basically a good boy. He wasn't the type to pressure me into having sex. Said he wanted to marry a virgin."

"Ah, honey," Dave mumbled into the cascade of auburn hair spread upon his pillow. Though he tightened his grip around her shoulders, his embrace remained infinitely tender.

"Does that mean Jason DeWinter was your first?"

Kayanne nodded against his shoulder. Suddenly she was sobbing for all the times she hadn't been able to shed a single tear. Like a dam giving way to years of neglect and building pressure, she crumbled and was swept away by the force of those memories.

"I should have decked that son of a bitch when I had the chance," Dave told her.

Kayanne was surprised by the vehemence of his reaction. She'd been waiting for him to do what everyone else in town had done at the time—blame her for Pete's death and call her a home wrecker. A slut without any morals whatsoever.

"Jason was young, too," she reminded him.

Dave's voice grew hard. "You might be willing to forgive that cretin, but I'm not. Downplay it all you want, but what he did was wrong. On many levels."

He leaned up on his elbow to look into her tear-streaked face. Kayanne did her best to focus on what he had to say and not the effect he had on her physically.

"None of it was your fault. You were a high-school student, and he was a counselor. He took advantage of you when you most needed adult guidance. The man should be in prison."

Kayanne put a hand on the hard plane of Dave's chest. "It was all such a long time ago," she said with a long-suffering sigh.

The last thing she needed in her life was more scandal. She remembered her mother sitting her down shortly after Pete's death and asking if she'd done anything to lead Mr. DeWinter on. Hearing that question spoken aloud by the one person who shouldn't have had to ask had sent Kayanne lurching out of the nest on wobbly, wet wings.

Looking back on her youth from the safety of Dave's cozy bed, she could analyze things more clearly than when her world had been caving in around her. Associating her lack of intimacy with Pete at least in part for why he killed himself, she had given herself to Jason as a form of penance. One that had sent her ricocheting from one bad relationship to another ever since.

Kayanne had trusted her father and Pete, both of whom had betrayed her by dying. Then she'd put her trust in Jason, who had used her and thrown her to the wolves. Was it any wonder she was commitment-phobic? In her mind, love was inexorably mixed up with death, deception and atonement, thus making her recent yearning for domesticity all the more confusing.

Moved by the fact that Dave, now knowing what he did, still felt the need to defend her, she considered the possibility that he might be different enough from other men to risk taking a chance on. The biggest problem was that all the romantic relationships she'd been in since high school had revolved around alcohol. Kayanne might be willing to put her battered heart on a platter one more time, but she could not afford to risk her hard-fought sobriety.

No matter how promising the relationship might be.

Or how wonderful the man might be.

It wasn't right to let Dave go on thinking that she'd played the part of the poor victim for the past decade. The night seemed made for confessions.

"Listen," she said, laying her history before Dave like a stained rug. "I don't want to mislead you. I'm no fair maiden who needs to be rescued from an ivory tower. I've been with lots of men since Jason DeWinter, and I don't think it's a good idea for you to run around trying to beat all of them up."

Kayanne held her breath waiting for him to explode. It wouldn't be the first time she'd left a man's bed with an oath on his lips. Forrester probably would have slapped her for such an antagonistic remark, but once again Dave proved to be cut from a finer cloth.

"You're right," he admitted, leaning down to kiss her on the lips. And cheeks. And earlobes. And on closed eyelids where, despite every attempt to push him away, Kayanne could not erase flickering images of spending the rest of her life with such a good and gentle man.

"First of all," he said, attempting to set the record straight, "I'm the one who needs to be rescued from an ivory tower. And secondly, now that you're with me, you can forget about those other men because they don't matter anymore."

Ten

Kayanne's heart soared like a kite far above the tedious fields where mere mortals played. Never could she have imagined Dave reacting to her candor in such a generous, high-minded fashion. Perhaps a second chance at love wasn't entirely out of the question for her after all. For one glittering moment, she walked up to the home of her dreams and peered right in the window. Tender images of living with this man, having his babies and sharing the rest of her life with him provided a glimpse of heaven on earth.

Then she spied that same bottle of whiskey that had been sitting half-empty on Dave's front porch the first time they'd met. Kayanne knew that just because she didn't want to drink anymore didn't mean Dave shouldn't be able to imbibe. History confirmed the fact that most of her favorite writers did their best work while under the influence, and she had no reason to believe that Dave was any different.

As much as Kayanne wanted to believe that she could be around other people who were drinking without slipping into dangerous old habits, she simply couldn't afford to trust herself so early in her recovery. The urge to drink was still strong in her, and she doubted it would ever completely go away. It had taken all of her willpower tonight just to resist temptation. Had Dave not been by her side at the reunion, she might have fallen off the wagon and landed face first in the spiked punch. It didn't take much of an imagination for her to envision a night that could have ended far differently.

Alcohol abuse was the reason she'd left Forrester, and Kayanne was convinced that if she wanted to maintain her sobriety, she would have to die an old maid. She wanted to believe that a woman could have a full and meaningful life without a man. Seeing Mrs. Rawlins again reassured her that being alone wasn't necessarily a bad thing. Satiated from mind-boggling sex and enjoying the warmth of Dave's strong body, however, Kayanne wasn't sure she wanted to live such a life.

It was important to weigh her present sense of euphoria against waking up clearheaded every morning. Nor could she dismiss the mysterious white light that had enveloped her when she'd forgiven Mr. DeWinter. Kayanne believed it to be a sign from God. Counting herself lucky not to have accidentally killed somebody before coming to her senses, she didn't want to risk stumbling back into her old life of missed appointments, meaningless relationships, drunk driving and fuzzy thinking.

As tempting as it might be to wrap herself in a lovely cotton-candy fantasy, Kayanne couldn't quite bring herself to believe in happily-ever-afters for people like her. Flesh-and-blood people who made awful mistakes that no amount of penitence could fix. Should she ever fall back into her old ways, the possibility of dragging Dave down with her was untenable. She never wanted him to regard her as she'd ultimately come to see Forrester—as a mean, hopeless drunk.

Dave lay in the dark with Kayanne in his arms and tears in his eyes. Long after her breath had ebbed to a steady rhythm, he continued stroking her hair. He couldn't have fashioned a more tragic history for her had he written it himself. Having crossed the line between fact and fiction, he could no more return to looking at her life objectively through a writer's microscope than he could turn his feelings on and off. He literally ached for her.

Kayanne made him want to be the man that she thought he was. A better man. The kind who could slay dragons and make her laugh at the same time.

If such expectations weren't reason enough to make him think twice about becoming more permanently involved with her, he also needed to remember that Kayanne came with a complete set of emotional baggage. Being a normal man however, that didn't seem to matter nearly as much to him as the fact that she also came like no one he'd ever known before. Fantasies of her in bed paled next to the real thing. A pure sexual being, Kayanne exuded passion with every breath she took, making it impossible for a naked man such as himself to think straight. It had been all he could do to keep from proposing to her when he'd climaxed.

The intensity of his emotions confounded him. It was unlike anything he'd ever felt before.

Why he felt the compulsion to protect this woman when it was clear to the entire world that he was the one who needed protection from her was beyond him. Of course, that didn't change the way he felt about her. Smart enough not to fight something as elemental as his body, Dave accepted that he had to have her. It was as simple as that.

His innate sense of optimism dawned as brightly as the sun the following day. Disheveled from a night of great sex and hard sleep, Kayanne looked beautiful in the early light. Dave bid her good morning over the plate of scrambled eggs and toast that he carried into the bedroom on a tray.

Sitting up and stretching, she asked, "What did I do to deserve such special treatment?"

Dave gave her a hungry look that had nothing to do with food. "You should know."

Taking a bite, she moaned with pleasure. "A girl could get used to this kind of treatment."

"That's the plan," he told her, wiggling his eyebrows maniacally.

Sitting beside her on the bed, he took her hand in his

and looked deeply in her eyes. "I have a question for you, sweetheart. And it's an important one."

Kayanne leaned back into her pillow as if preparing herself for the worst. She put down her fork and said, "You have my full attention."

Dave took a deep breath and speared her with a sizzling gaze.

"Would you consider moving in with me?"

Kayanne nearly choked on her toast.

When she'd been a little girl, her mother had drilled into her that disgusting old analogy about a man not buying the cow if the milk were free. Even now, as a grown liberated woman, she associated premarital sex with a subsequent breakup. Even though she wasn't exactly looking to get married any time soon, the thought of cohabitating with such a sexy roommate held a whole lot more appeal than spending nights watching game shows with her mother. Her newfound closeness with Suzanne was wearing thin under the constant proximity of living in a fifteen-by-seventy-foot trailer. If last night proved anything at all, it was that Kayanne was tired of sleeping alone.

Totally ignoring the emotional costs, she ran the logistics through her mind. If she moved in with Dave, she'd still be close enough to check in on her mother while allowing her the opportunity to adjust gradually to independent living. Regardless of where her relationship with Dave led, Kayanne wasn't planning on living with her mother forever. Eventually, she intended to pick up her modeling career where it had left off. Full throttle.

Getting hooked up with a hopeless romantic wasn't any way to advance her career goals, but something inside Kayanne assured her that was the right thing to do.

"This is sudden," she pointed out, not wanting to ruin something so perfect by rushing things.

"The heart knows what it wants," was Dave's sage reply. "And I want you."

"I want you, too," Kayanne admitted.

More than anyone else she'd ever met. She wondered if it would surprise Dave to know she'd never lived with another man. For her, sex was one thing. And commitment was quite another.

"I'll take the day off from work tomorrow, and we'll start moving your stuff in right away," Dave said, taking charge of the situation.

Kayanne held up both hands. Heat rushed to her face. As much as she hated to, it was time to put a pin in this hot-air balloon before it set sail for Destination Heartache.

"Hold on. Before you go getting the cart before the horse, there's one more thing I should tell you."

In spite of the fact that she'd had lots of practice admitting her problem to other alcoholics at AA meetings, she found the words extremely difficult to get out. Once Dave heard her out, she expected him to rescind the offer. She toyed with the edge of her sheet, wishing there were some way of softening the ugly truth.

"I'm a lush," she said, averting her eyes from his.

The fact that Dave didn't act all that surprised set Kayanne back some.

"That might be a bit harsh, considering that I've

never seen you take a drink—even though last night you had to be tempted," he pointed out.

She started to argue, but Dave cut off any further protests by covering her mouth with his and proceeding to convince her without words why she'd be a fool to turn him down. Once she felt as limber as a rag doll in his arms, he did his best to reassure her.

"We'll work it out. Between the two of us, there isn't any obstacle we can't conquer. You just have to be willing to ask for my help. And accept it when it's offered."

That he neither dismissed her illness nor turned away in disgust was nothing short of miraculous. A rush of gratitude filled Kayanne's heart and spilled over in the breaking light of day as she contemplated the power of hope. Physically and emotionally spent, she thought she had no more passion to give.

She was wrong.

Dave caressed her cheek with the knuckles of one hand. The other sought the cleft between her legs where the glow of awareness rekindled the blaze that he'd started earlier. Intimacy arched between them.

He tested her willpower with the tip of his tongue against the seam of her lips. Reaching behind herself, Kayanne grabbed the brass bars of the headboard with both hands and gave herself over to the pure pleasure of being dominated by a man who knew exactly what he was doing.

He rolled on top of her, nudging her legs apart with his own. His mouth grew more demanding. His kisses more intense as he plied her with his tongue and plunged the depth of her mouth at will. Trailing his fingertips along her rib cage, his hands settled at last upon her waist, lifting her up so that she had no choice but to feel the extent of his arousal against her belly.

Moaning, she kneaded her fingertips into his muscles growing slicker by the minute with beads of sweat. Dave ran his hands down her buttocks and drew her possessively against himself. Staring deeply into her eyes, he entered her in a sudden thrust that gave voice to her pleasure in guttural, nonsensical syllables. She threw back her head and gave herself fully to him.

He filled her completely. Physically, emotionally, spiritually. Kayanne knew that she'd never find a more satisfying fit if she searched the world over. She clung to him in both desperation and faith.

Dave took a labored breath.

"Say yes," he commanded through gritted teeth. "Say that you'll move in with me."

Kayanne flexed her hips against his, urging him to succumb to the need to climax quickly. Unable to wait a second longer herself, she gave him the answer he longed to hear before exploding into a million shining shards of bliss. "Yes, oh, yes!"

Only then did Dave pour himself into her, sealing their bodies tight and calling out her name as if flinging a plea heavenward.

Spiraling back to her senses an eternity later, Kayanne came to the conclusion that nothing had ever felt as right as her decision to be with this man for as long as he wanted to be with her. It was pointless to doubt his goodness. After everything she'd told him, after all that he'd heard by way of nasty innuendo and gossip, he was still willing to take a chance on her. Only a saint could resist such stubborn determination. And everyone in town knew that Kayanne was no saint.

Nor was she a coward.

A woman who would rather live with mistakes than regrets, she was bound to her word—even if it was given in the throes of orgasm. Savoring the feeling of closeness that being in this man's arms brought her, she snuggled up against him and let a sense of contentment wash over her. If it were in her power, she'd never move again.

"There's just one more thing," she mumbled against the strong column of his neck.

"What now?"

Dave sounded incredulous that there could possibly be anything else to disclose before committing to their new living arrangements.

Kayanne's voice was only half-teasing when she posed a final question. "How are we going to break the news to Rose?"

Having things all worked out in his mind, Dave was feeling good about life as he moved Kayanne's meager belongings from her mother's trailer into his spacious home. During the day, Kayanne would be away at work, unconsciously providing the impetus to move his plot along. And during the night, they could pleasure one another like there was no tomorrow.

Loading the last of her boxes into the back of his

SUV, he refused to dwell on the possibility that Kayanne may very well grow tired of playing the penitent and go back to her glamorous lifestyle. If that happened, Dave supposed he could always resume his boring old life with stuffy colleagues and dusty manuscripts. Worse yet, if he couldn't make his writing pay off on a more regular and substantial basis, he imagined himself working for the family firm receiving transfusions of ink to replace the blood that Kayanne made boil with a simple look.

In spite of his previous glib response, Dave took very seriously the acknowledgment that she was an alcoholic. Kayanne hadn't been particularly coy about dropping hints about making amends early on in their relationship, and he'd noticed that she never drank in his presence. Having simply assumed she was a teetotaler, he'd been taken aback when she'd hinted at stopping by a bar rather than going to the reunion.

Dave couldn't help but wonder what effect her condition would have on his own life. While he didn't consider himself a problem drinker, he did occasionally oil the creative pump with a cocktail or a beer, and the thought of going cold turkey didn't much appeal to him.

Would it be all right if he had a drink in her presence?

Would she think he was trying to sabotage her efforts?

The last thing Dave wanted to do was jeopardize Kayanne's sobriety. He'd always taken for granted his ability to drink without fully realizing what a blessing it was to be able to stop at one or two. He hated the thought of sneaking a highball behind her back.

He wondered what his parents would make of someone as complex as Kayanne. His normally reserved
mother maintained that familiarity bred contempt. If
that was truly the case, the living arrangements he'd
proposed might well prove a fairly painless tonic to the
romantic inclinations that were interfering with any pre-
sumption of logical thought. Every minute of the day
and night he could think of little else but Kayanne. She
was an obsession that threatened to take over not just
his storyline, but his whole life.

If Dave wasn't careful, he suspected he might not
fare any better than poor Jasmine, who'd paid the ultimate price shortly after Kayanne had stepped onto his
porch. However unrealistic it was to think he could survive living in close quarters with nothing more than a
nick or two to his big old compassionate heart, it was a
risk he felt he had to take.

Life with Dave was filled not only with passion, but
also lots of fun. Having grown up in a home seeped in the
odor of perpetual grief, Kayanne's early existence had
been marked by a frugality of both the pocketbook and
the heart. Tender words were as rare in the Aldarmann
house as disposable cash. Thus she had fallen in more
easily with men like Forrester, who were prone to melo-
dramatic bursts of angst and wild spending, than men
like Dave, who smiled easily and often at simple things.

His generosity of spirit even extended to his closet.
He acted surprised that she'd actually brought so little
along in terms of personal effects.

"Over the years I've learned to travel light," Kayanne said, subtly warning him in advance that he might very well come home someday to find her gone.

But Dave wasn't an easy man to pick a fight with. In response, he simply squirted a whiff of her expensive perfume in the air and took a deep breath.

"I like the fact that you've made a conscious decision to acquire only the very best rather than fill your life with junk," he said.

Kayanne wondered if he was referring to past lovers rather than things as inconsequential as jewelry and fragrances. Recalling all the cheap relationships she'd thrown into junk drawers in the past, Kayanne thought this fresh-faced, smiling Adonis deserved someone less jaded to share the sunshine of his optimism. She didn't want to leave Dave feeling as depleted as men such as Forrester had left her.

When she attempted to underscore the fact that their living arrangements were only temporary, Dave refused to listen. Instead, he turned up the stereo and danced her to the bedroom, where he kissed such foreboding thoughts away, reminding her with each loving caress to enjoy the here and now rather than dwell on future miseries. Accustomed to using sex as a weapon, Kayanne found herself befuddled when it was used so masterfully against her.

Generally speaking, life with Dave proved to be a picnic. Weekends and evenings were spent hiking, biking, bowling and playing tennis. Every so often he even coaxed her down to the basement to lift some light weights in his makeshift gym. Nights were spent exhausting one another in pleasures of the flesh far after all the late, late shows signed off. Not that Kayanne kept track of such things. Unlike her mother's trailer where the blare of the television filtered into every room twenty-four hours a day, the TV was seldom turned on in her new home.

One promising Saturday morning after staying in bed until the sun could no longer be restrained by the blinds, Dave suggested a camping trip. Picturing herself as some dark, Gothic maiden imprinted implausibly upon a Currier and Ives scene, Kayanne laughed at the absurdity of it before agreeing to go.

On their way out of town, they stopped by the grocery store to pick up a six-pack of cold pop. Dave promised a mess of fish for dinner, and Kayanne had made dessert herself—chunky chocolate-chip cookies the size of his fist. She enjoyed filling the house with the aroma of comfort foods that had been off-limits for so long in her line of work. Participation in Dave's active lifestyle allowed her to consume all the calories she wanted without worrying about weight gain. The unexpected freedom was a slice of heaven.

"Delicious," Dave told her as she fed him cookies on the way up the mountain.

Kayanne was gratified when he raved how good they were. Grabbing her by the wrist, he ignored her protests and sucked melted chocolate from her fingertips.

"Just a precursor of things to come," he promised.

A flame licked between her thighs. Generated from

a white heat, the fire burned hotter and cleaner than any ignited from the desperate desire that had been extinguished so easily in past relationships.

They thoroughly enjoyed each other's company and the scenery as they drove to the picturesque Cloud Peak Wilderness. There, Dave wasted no time assembling his new fly rod. Kayanne whistled in appreciation when he stripped off his sweatshirt to exchange it for a cooler T-shirt. Grinning, he gave her his best beefcake-calendar pose.

"You're pretty buff for an academic," she told him, resting her chin in her hands and admiring the view from the blanket she'd spread on the ground.

Rolling onto her back, she studied an ideal Wyoming summer sky. Ribbons of wispy clouds floated across a blue so bright it warranted sunglasses. Squinting, Kayanne tried to remember the last time she'd been so happy. The answer came to her in a single word. *Never.*

Dave asked her to spray him with a fine mist of mosquito repellent, which she did before handing him a bottle of sunscreen.

"Mind returning the favor?" she asked.

Kayanne was wearing cutoffs and a flowered-print halter top that brought out a softer shade of green in a pair of eyes that Dave said reminded him of aspen leaves in the springtime. Kayanne held her long mane of hair out of the way as his hands rubbed liquid sunshine into her skin. He lingered along the swell of her breasts where they peeked out from the sides of her top.

"There's not a soul around," he murmured into her

ear before slipping his hands under the halter to fondle their ripe fullness.

Kayanne neither chastised nor pushed him away. Instead, she arched her spine and let her head fall back, catching strands of her hair in the sticky lotion not yet absorbed into her skin. The next thing she knew, Dave was untying the knot at the nape of her neck and nuzzling the hollow between her neck and shoulder blade. Reveling in the sensation of being so thoroughly fondled, she wondered if this wasn't what it must have been like for Adam and Eve before they were tossed out of paradise. Isolated from the rest of the world, Kayanne felt no shame being half-undressed in the warm sunshine.

Sighing, Dave regretfully retied her top. "I'd better get fishing before the sun goes down."

Kayanne donned an artful little pout. "Are you sure I can't tempt you to stay a little longer?"

"If I don't catch dinner, I won't have any energy left to do to you later what I promised I would."

He emphasized his point by covering his hard-on with an old fishing hat decorated with an assortment of flies and lures.

"Looks like you already caught a whopper," Kayanne teased.

She declined his offer to accompany him to the stream, saying she'd rather read a steamy novel to get her in the mood for what was to come later—that was, if he could be counted on to keep his promises. Beaming, he took off. Kayanne surveyed him through heavy eyelids. Wearing a pair of khaki shorts and an old, battered hat, he looked better than any airbrushed boy toy of her past.

The scent of pine filled her with a rare sense of belonging. Home at last in these sacred mountains, her spirit sang with the rushing river. She dozed in the midst of a meadow so thick with wild sunflowers that it looked as though it had been painted with butter. When she opened her eyes an hour or so later, Dave was standing over her with a stringer of trout. He couldn't have looked any prouder presenting her with a world-record trophy sailfish.

"Dinner," he announced, puffing his chest out in his best caveman imitation. "Breakfast, too, for that matter."

Drops of water slid off the fish's tail onto Kayanne's bare ankle. She bolted upright with a girlish squeal.

"I didn't know you were such a sissy," Dave said with a disapproving shake of his head.

"If you want to see real panic, just wait until a bear wanders into camp."

The revelation that he kept a .44 Magnum stashed away in the glove box for just such emergencies helped allay her concerns. That evening, they roasted s'mores over an open campfire and fed them to one another as if sampling the finest aphrodisiacs. And perhaps they were—if what followed shortly thereafter in the confines of a down sleeping bag was any indication.

Falling asleep beneath a canopy of stars twinkling overhead was a dizzying experience. It was like falling into the universe's mixing bowl. Kayanne felt something hard inside her chest crack open as the healing that had begun with an act of forgiveness and an amazing white light continued to work its magic into the farthest reaches of her soul.

Eleven

Unlike her more religious mother, Kayanne didn't believe in signs from God in the form of stray pennies found on the ground or randomly turning to just the right bible verse for whatever ailed a person in times of need. She didn't prescribe to the notion that AIDS was a sign of God's displeasure with the world. Or in any of the splashy headlines about the fulfillment of Nostradamus's end-of-the-world predictions with every natural disaster.

Nevertheless, on the way home from her first camping trip, giddy with a newfound sense of joy, it was hard to dismiss the possibility that God just might be trying to tell her something. Coming out of the foothills of the Big Horn Mountains, a lone antelope stepped into the middle of the road and forced their vehicle to come to a complete stop. The buck deliberately turned his head to look straight at Kayanne, making it impossible to miss the black lacquered heart that his horns formed above his head. Squeezing Dave's hand, she hoped she wasn't the only one to read the magic into the incident.

Of course, she told herself that if she bought into that kind of superstitious nonsense, she'd also have to assume the storm sweeping across the skyline in an ominous curtain of dark, swollen clouds was a portent of things to come as well. When the lowest lying of those clouds caught on the ragged tips of mountaintops and spilled their fury upon a panorama virtually untouched by human hands since the inception of time, Kayanne couldn't help but shiver with a chilling sense of foreboding.

If Dave shared her sense of apprehension, he didn't show it. Ever since she'd burst into his life like a storm on the horizon, he'd felt happier than ever before. Life was suddenly wonderful. The colors of the sunrise made their way onto his pages and into his heart. As did the splash of raindrops against the window. And the smell of fresh cut grass. He heard himself whistling at odd times, glad to be carving out the life he wanted on his own terms. The smothering job awaiting him in the steamy South receded to a distant possibility instead of the crushing likelihood it had seemed just a few short weeks ago.

Kayanne was present in everything he did. Not satisfied with killing off Jasmine to supplant her as the leading lady in his book, she took over his thoughts as well.

Every heroine in every book Dave read became her. It didn't matter whether the author was describing a short blonde or a delicate brunette; in his mind's eye, she was a feisty redhead with cat-green eyes and a heart of gold.

His own book was coming along fine, and he didn't even miss liquor as he'd first thought he might. It had felt strange pouring himself a plain soda when it came time for a break from writing, but as the words began to flow onto the page almost effortlessly, without the aid of alcohol, he accepted the fact that Kayanne was all the inspiration he needed. Day after day, his fingers flew over the keyboard as he struck a rhythm that didn't allow time for the painstaking revision that had marked his past efforts.

His prose took on a more sensual, expansive tone as she taught him to look at the world differently. The wanton character who had so shamelessly taunted his hero at the start of his book became softer and more complex with each new chapter. Perhaps because of her faults and mysterious past, Dave knew his readers could no more resist falling in love with her than he could himself.

A meticulous author who tended to labor over every word, Dave was frankly uncomfortable with where this raging torrent of prose was taking him. But after weeks of struggling to get so much as a single paragraph down to his satisfaction, he simply buckled himself in as Spice took the driver's seat and headed for an unknown destination. That wasn't to say that Dave considered every word golden, only that he accepted there would be time enough for revision after his first draft was completed.

His project was coming along so well in fact that he felt no remorse in turning off his computer every day the minute Kayanne came home from her shift. Rather than admit to hiding anything from her, he considered spending the rest of his day playing with her a reward for a day's hard work. He supposed that was what had been missing from his writing all along: a sense of balance that only such a woman could bring to his life. It would be too easy for someone of his nature to bury himself in his work, cut himself off from life with other academics and offset his growing loneliness with a strenuous physical lifestyle. Perhaps that was why he'd chosen the least populous of the fifty states to settle down and write his next novel in virtual obscurity. Maybe he secretly subscribed to the notion that only tortured, lonely lives could spawn great literature.

Possibly that was why he kept a lone bottle of whiskey secreted away in the back of his cupboard just in case his newfound inspiration failed him. All the rest he'd poured down the drain—over Kayanne's protests.

"You don't have to do that on my account," she'd told him. "I'm the one with the problem, not you."

Dave had lightly brushed off her concern. "It won't hurt me any to clean up my life right along with you. I like feeling less tied to the bottle myself."

The indulgent smile Kayanne had given him had made him feel naive. His idea of being addicted was clearly much different than hers. A heavy weight that he vaguely recognized as jealousy had slowly begun to crush his spirit. It was an emotion he credited only to the pettiest characters in both the books that he read and wrote. He did his best not to think about Kayanne's past, pushing aside any nagging doubts he might have. Though he avoided prying into her past beyond what she'd already told him, it bothered him to think about the men that she had been with before him. The thought of Kayanne leaving him for some glamorous playboy who knew his way around a camera played havoc with his guts.

Forget it, you'll make yourself crazy. What's in the past doesn't matter as much as what's in the here and now.

He freely admitted that Kayanne wasn't like anyone he'd ever brought home to meet his parents. Fiery and passionate, there was also a delicate side to her that few people saw. Laughter didn't come easily to her, but when she tossed back her magnificent mane of hair and let go of her inhibitions, the sound was pure music. And the fact that she was starting to trust him allowed that wondrous sound to fill his home more and more often.

Although Kayanne believed that she would never ever completely conquer her desire for alcohol, she was down to attending an AA meeting once a week. She always returned home calmer and more grounded than when she'd left. And she never failed to thank him for his part in her continued sobriety.

Dave was both touched and frightened by that. He was equally moved by the way she fretted over her clients, especially Rose, who still made an occasional appearance on his front porch. She hadn't quite forgiven Kayanne for stealing her man. That bothered Kayanne more than anyone might imagine. Only Dave knew how

hard she was trying to find Rose a more age-appropriate companion. And to liven up the stifling atmosphere
over at the Evening Star Manor for all the residents for
whom she was coming to care so deeply.

In her spare time, Kayanne devoted herself to designing a new line of clothing geared to older buyers. Dave
was duly impressed with her plans. She didn't want to
jinx things by being overconfident, but all it had taken
to get the ball rolling was a few well-placed calls to her
fashion contacts in Manhattan.

"I wish you'd quit your job and focus on your designs
full-time," Dave told her. "There are lots of ways to
help your friends and make better use of your talents in
the process."

Kayanne gave him a tired smile. "As much as I appreciate your support, I really can't resign until I have
the backers to turn my designs into something more
than a pipe dream."

Dave suspected it was more than that. Kayanne's
current paycheck might not be much, but it kept her from
feeling completely dependent on him. Even though she
trusted him more and more each day, he committed
himself to a gradual process of winning her over completely. So when he offered her money in support of her
dream, he tried not to take her refusal personally.

She was more open to other kinds of help.

"Good news," he announced one evening after she'd
just hung up the phone with a local seamstress who'd
volunteered to sew samples of her designs. Kayanne
was hoping to take them to the center and do an informal

market analysis herself. "I think I met somebody today who just might be perfect for Rose."

Kayanne looked at him hopefully. She was so frustrated with the local pool of eligible men that she had even considered hooking Rose up via an Internet dating service.

"Does he have a pulse?" was all she wanted to know.

"His name is Joe Hansen. He works at Wallyworld as the greeter. Been retired for years and went back to work to keep busy. Says he'd rather wear out than rust out. Heck of a nice guy."

Kayanne was so encouraged by this news flash that she proceeded to show her gratitude by scattering kisses on Dave's neck and slowly working her way down his chest. She undid his top shirt button with her teeth before allowing him to do the rest.

"You're awfully tough on my shirts," he told her in a voice that let her know he didn't mind at all.

After divesting him of his shirt, Kayanne opened her own blouse and gently directed his head down to the hollow between her breasts where he greedily indulged. She didn't have to stroke him to make him as hard as a rock, but she did anyway, and in the fading light of day proceeded to satisfy him completely right in the middle of the living-room floor. Spilling into her, Dave gave every ounce of his entire being to her: marrow, bone, flesh, blood, memories, hopes and dreams. Their lovemaking transcended the physical to reach a higher plane where soul met soul beneath slick, hot flesh.

Dave knew that there would probably always be places inside Kayanne that he'd never be able to touch.

But when she curled up beside him naked on the rug in front of a cold fireplace and smiled at him, he rejoiced to see the wounded look in her eyes was gone. He never wanted to be responsible for putting that look back on her face again.

Luckily, Kayanne didn't have to wait for the bookstore to call with information on her ordered copy of Dave's first book. One day while cleaning, she found a copy unobtrusively stuck on his bookshelf. She read it all in one sitting but didn't bother to mention it to him later because it had left her feeling so sad. His words were like poetry on the page, but the scenes he painted of the South—dripping magnolia blossoms, gracious living and the rich loam of dirt stained by the blood of a civil war—made her feel separate from the man whose bed she shared. His beautiful words divided their two worlds as neatly as a math problem and reminded Kayanne that they were from as different backgrounds and experiences as one could imagine.

Wondering if she was having any impact on his writing at all, she hoped that his latest work in progress lacked the elegant aloofness that marked that first novel. Kayanne wanted his next hero to be characterized more by genuine love and less by longing for the kind of woman who existed only in the fantasy world of the male ego. And she wanted a heroine to relate to as well. Someone of flesh and bone with an interesting past and enough flaws to make her worth cheering for. Someone she didn't resent for perfectly coifed blond hair, neatly manicured nails and impeccable manners. In short, Kayanne wanted somebody real to read and care about.

And she wanted a happy ending, too. Not the kind of depressing conclusion that pandered more to literary critics than avid readers like herself. She wasn't looking for some gossamer ending that implied there would be no bumps on the road beyond the last page, but if Kayanne was going to invest her time reading a book, she wanted a satisfying conclusion that gave her hope of finding lasting love herself.

A closet romantic, she didn't want to discuss Dave's first book with him for fear of appearing jealous of a fictional woman that she detested. Besides, whenever she asked to see his latest project, he always found some way to put her off. She noticed that he never worked on his book when she was around, always taking care to shut down his laptop completely whenever she was in the room.

Kayanne supposed he was entitled to be protective of his work, but that didn't do a thing to lessen her curiosity. In fact, it only heightened her desire to see what he was writing so diligently while she was off at her job. She didn't know his password and would never have violated his privacy by trying to break into his files, but when the day came that she stumbled upon a printed draft of the first few chapters, she didn't talk herself out of reading them, either.

Dave was at the college setting up his office, so there was no reason to rush through the stack of papers while looking over her shoulder. If the chapters were good, she would casually mention it to him before kissing him senseless and making him forget all about any little breach of privacy on her part. If they weren't, she'd keep her disappointment to herself and kiss him senseless anyway.

They were good.

Good enough to make her long for the smooth bite of liquor to erase his cruel, poignant words from her mind forever.

Kayanne felt blindsided. All this time, she'd been under the impression that Dave actually had tender feelings for her beyond what they shared physically. Having fallen hopelessly in love with him, she was embarrassed that in weak moments she'd actually allowed herself to consider the ultimate fantasy of marrying him and having his children.

All the while he'd been playing her for a fool.

She'd never met a more calculating person in her whole life than this man with his lying, generous smile and magical hands. The whole time she had been falling for Dave like some stupid schoolgirl, he had been standing back, observing, and putting every unflattering, minute detail of her so-called life down on paper.

Laughing at her.

One didn't have to be a genius to see how he had connected her to his trampy female protagonist. It didn't take a great leap of the imagination to link their names together, either. Or the fact that they shared the same red hair, green eyes and questionable pasts. Dave captured perfectly on the page the way Kayanne walked and talked and mistreated his poor, suffering hero—some stupid SOB who kept mooning over a Barbie doll by the name of Jasmine.

Kayanne read only to the end of the scene where she found herself implicated in Jasmine's death before putting the manuscript down in disgust. She didn't think she could suffer through the love scenes, seeing her heart and her legs splayed for the entire world to gawk at. Having been taught to guard her heart by some of the best con men in the business, Kayanne chastised herself for not seeing this treachery coming long ago.

Hurt, embarrassed and angry, she baptized the next *New York Times* bestseller with the flow of hot tears. Then promised herself it would be the last time she cried over a man. This particular one would damn well never see her tears. Forrester might have scared and humiliated her with his fist, but the emotional blow Dave delivered was far more crippling. For Kayanne, trusting him at all had been a tremendous leap of faith.

Out there in the big old cold world, she'd encountered many men like Jason DeWinter and Forrester who all wanted something from her. Prestige, money, contacts, sex. Those were things Kayanne could understand, if not accept. But this? How was she to deal with a literary rape that left her feeling more violated than any physical act of violence? How was she supposed to compete with another woman who was made of nothing but words? It wounded her to think that all the while she'd been making love to Dave, he had been dissecting her performance right along with her motives. And judging her.

Never had Kayanne been more insulted and hurt in her entire life. And she'd had more than her fair share of humiliating experiences from which to draw a comparison.

A literary whore, she felt dirty. She kicked the coffee table and screamed. She tore at her hair. And when she was done, she felt gutted. But no closer to knowing how to proceed than before venting all her emotions on an empty room.

Should she confront Dave when he walked through the front door by waving the evidence in his face?

Should she burn it? Light up the old fireplace, toast marshmallows over his laptop, and let him try to reconstruct his precious masterpiece by memory?

Perhaps sue him for libel?

Knowing it wouldn't be wise to rush into any decision feeling the way she did right now, Kayanne reached for an old friend as she headed for the cupboard where Dave had a bottle of whiskey with her name on it stashed away.

"Anybody home?"

Dave's voice echoed through the house. Although he'd done it for years, he hated coming home to an empty house. He'd easily gotten used to being welcomed home by a woman whose eyes lit up the instant he hit the front door. Breathing in the scent of homemade minestrone soup simmering in a Crock-Pot, he marveled anew at the fact that Kayanne took such pleasure from cooking for him. Nothing could have pleased him more than seeing his supermodel lover immersed in domestic bliss. Just watching her bend over his long-neglected flower garden was enough to send him into erotic fantasies.

"Honey, I'm home," he said, acknowledging how that old chestnut characterized every man's need to make his presence known in his own home.

The silence that met this announcement was unnerving. Usually Kayanne came running to give him a big hug and make him feel like the king of his humble castle. Today the only sound that greeted him was the clock on the mantel chiming out the hours. Three o'clock on a Saturday and no sign of Kayanne.

Something was terribly wrong.

Loneliness blew through Dave like a cold blast of wind. Where was she? He wondered how he could have grown so accustomed to her presence that even a short absence filled him with such a horrible sense of emptiness. He looked around for a note informing him of her whereabouts.

Nothing.

Just an open cupboard door.

A trickle of sweat ran down his neck at the realization that that was where he kept the only bottle of booze in the house.

"Please no."

Swallowing hard, Dave called out her name. His imagination raced faster than his feet as he searched the house room to room starting with the bedroom.

Maybe she'd taken ill and was just resting.

Maybe she was pregnant and didn't even know it

yet. Maybe he'd have to be the one to point out the signs of morning sickness to her. He'd been careful about using condoms, but Dave knew there were worse things than fathering children with the most beautiful woman on earth. The very thought puffed him up with sudden pride. He wondered how Kayanne felt about children. Surely she wouldn't do away with an unborn child without his knowledge.

Taking the steps by twos, Dave considered what kind of father he would be. Hopefully not one who would force his child into a profession he didn't love. Nor one whose judgment might cause his children to hesitate about marrying the love of their life simply because of differences in social backgrounds.

Get a grip on yourself, he told himself. *You're making yourself crazy for no reason.*

He'd never given much thought to marriage before. Just committing to living together had been a gigantic step for a man who placed a high value on his privacy and independence.

Dave threw the bedroom door open. The room was empty. Completely empty of any sign that Kayanne had ever been there at all.

Her things were gone. Her clothes and jewelry and fascinating, feminine fragrances.

All gone.

Dave hadn't thought it possible to miss the sight of cosmetics taking up space on his bathroom counter, but at that moment there wasn't anything he owned that he wouldn't have traded for such a comforting nuisance.

He sat down on the edge of the bed and faced the awful truth. Kayanne had left him.

Just like that.

Without so much as an explanation.

She'd warned him that she traveled light in case the urge to move on ever struck, but it had never occurred to Dave that she'd vanish without even saying goodbye. Telling himself that something must have happened, that she must have been called away unexpectedly, he imagined the worst. Her mother had taken ill again and she was at the hospital. Giving blood. Or Rose was on her deathbed demanding to see Kayanne so she could make peace with her before crossing over.

Dave knew that it must be a sin to wish for a catastrophe just to provide a legitimate reason for Kayanne's disappearance, but he didn't care. He'd take any thread of hope offered. Swamped by panic, he played the events of the day over and over again in his head. Had he said something to upset her? Done something insensitive? Not done something that he should have done?

Had Forrester returned to carry her away on a magnificent black Harley-Davidson motorcycle with the promise of more wild, exciting times? Dave pictured Kayanne's long hair blowing in the wind as she snuggled up against Forrester's leather-clad back, both of them laughing at the idea of her ever settling down with anyone as ordinary as a college English professor. Acid poured into Dave's stomach, eating him up from the inside out.

There's got to be a logical explanation. She wouldn't do this to me. She just wouldn't.

But all Dave knew for sure was that Kayanne was gone. And he couldn't imagine life without her. Determined to track her to the ends of the earth if he had to, he went in search of clues. It didn't take him long to find one in his office: an open bottle of Jack Daniel's whiskey with an empty glass and an AA token next to it.

A sinking feeling caught him off guard, causing him to stumble. Looking down, he recognized a page from his manuscript at his feet. He bent down and examined it. It was from the chapter in which he'd first introduced Spice. Swearing, Dave crushed his own words into a ball and launched it across the room. Remedying this terrible mistake wouldn't be nearly as easy as pressing the delete key.

Twelve

When Kayanne showed up on her mother's doorstep unexpectedly, she discovered an unlikely ally in Suzanne Aldarmann. She took one look at her daughter's face, enfolded her in a hug and welcomed her back home. What surprised Kayanne even more than the rare display of physical affection was the fact that her mother didn't press for any details. She simply put on a pot of coffee and helped her move back into her old room. It was a process that didn't take long.

"Do you want to talk about it?"

"I don't think I can, Mom. Not yet." Kayanne swallowed hard. "Maybe never."

Suzanne patted her hand. "It's never easy watching

your child suffer heartache, and you've certainly had your fair share, honey."

It was funny how much that simple acknowledgment meant to Kayanne. Her throat closed around a solid lump.

"I'd hoped this one was different," Suzanne said, taking care to avoid mentioning Dave's name specifically.

"That's the trouble," Kayanne explained. "He was."

Her mother handed her an entire box of tissues, stared straight into her daughter's eyes and cut to the heart of the matter. "You've got it bad, don't you?"

If AA had taught Kayanne anything, it was that she had to be honest with herself. After a lifetime of keeping secrets from her mother, she admitted with a sigh, "I love him, Mom."

Suzanne put an arm around her daughter's shoulders and commiserated. "You poor thing."

Kayanne supposed she hadn't shared much about her romantic relationships with her mother for fear of shocking her. Mostly because in the past those relationships had been more about sex than love. Suzanne was far more qualified to discuss the latter, having considerable personal experience in dealing with the loss of her one true love and none in filling the void her husband's death left with meaningless relationships.

"Have you told him that you love him?" Suzanne asked gently.

"No, thank God."

Not in words anyway.

That, at least, was something for which to be grateful. Kayanne couldn't bear the thought of those three little words making it onto the pages of Dave's manuscript in some mocking manner. Especially considering that she'd never said them to another man except her father.

Since there was nothing more that could be said that wouldn't belabor her broken heart, the two women worked together in silence for the remainder of the afternoon, each tending their separate memories. Kayanne was making room for her suitcase in the back of her closet when she came across an old box of memorabilia.

"It's some of your old awards, report cards and diaries that I've been saving for you," her mother said. She held up her hands to ward off an attack. "Don't worry, I didn't read any of them."

Kayanne was glad. What good could come from rummaging through the hurts of the past—unless it was to put the pain of the present into perspective? She'd survived her father's death, her first sweetheart's suicide, a disastrous relationship with a married man and countless ill-fated flings, including an ongoing one with alcohol. None of them matched the intensity of the anguish she felt over Dave using her.

When a sharp rap on the door made her jump, she told her mother in no uncertain terms, "If it's Dave, tell him that I'm not here."

Suzanne didn't argue. She just quietly went to answer the door, leaving her daughter alone to sort out her things and her thoughts. Five minutes later, Dave filled the doorway with his broad shoulders. Kayanne couldn't imagine what he'd said to smooth talk his way past her mother, but she wasn't pleased to see him. That

in spite of the way her heart leaped to her throat threatening to divulge her body's treachery.

"Well, if it isn't 'Enry 'Iggins come to make a respectable lady out of a poor flower girl. You'd best set the good
china, Mum, for me gentleman caller," she hollered in her
best Eliza Doolittle imitation before her voice turned
sharply bitter. "And I do use that term loosely."

"She's not here," Dave said. "Your mother was gracious enough to give us some privacy to work through
our problems ourselves."

Afraid of falling back into his tender gaze and never
being able to find her way back home, she deflected her
gaze. Abandoned by the one woman in the world whose
support she should have been able to count on, Kayanne
dropped all pretense of good manners.

"What is it you want?"

Her bedroom was so small that Dave could touch
both walls at the same time if he chose to. Knowing how
dangerous it was being confined in such a small place
with him, she considered rushing the door to escape.
The likelihood was that such foolish action would
simply land her on her back upon the old twin bed. And
if the bed didn't break beneath their combined weight,
Kayanne feared that her willpower would. She couldn't
bear the thought of the humble little room that had nur-
tured her childhood dreams finding its way onto the
pages of Dave's next novel.

"First and foremost I came to see if you're okay."

Kayanne rolled her eyes. "By okay do you mean if
I'm out 'indiscriminately cavorting with a string of

second-rate lovers'?" she asked, quoting a line directly from his work in progress.

Dave winced to hear his own words thrown in his face. "I mean okay as in sober."

Kayanne was blunt. "What do you care? Don't let the fact that you haven't found me drinking myself to death in the gutter keep you from using it in your book."

Dave's face darkened. He reached out to place the pad of his thumb under her chin and tipped her head, forcing her to look at him.

"Whatever you think of me right now, don't ever doubt that I care a great deal about you."

Kayanne jerked her head away. How could he possibly manage to sound so sincere all the while twisting the knife deeper into her back?

"If you ever get tired of writing, you've got a great career ahead of you as an actor," she told him. "It sure as hell takes a flair for the dramatic to waltz in here pretending concern when all you're really doing is scoping out more sordid details for your next chapter."

She grabbed a diary out of the box she'd been sorting through and launched it at him. It bounced off his head.

"Maybe you can find some dirt in there from my junior-high days that might be useful in developing a misbegotten gutter snipe as a foil for your perfect heroine."

Dave rubbed his forehead. "Now listen—"

"No, you listen," she said, taking as careful aim with her words as with the diary she'd fired at him. "I'm just fine. A little hurt and worse for wear. And, yes, to address your concerns, I did have to think long and hard about having a drink after reading your true opinion of me. But after careful consideration, I decided you weren't worth it."

Kayanne read the relief in Dave's face. And the hurt. Pouring that glass of whiskey down the drain had been one of the hardest things she'd ever done. The smell alone had almost been enough to push her over the edge. Her white-light revelation hadn't taken away her desire for alcohol, but it had given her the strength to defy her demons. Given the circumstances, that was as close to a miracle as she could hope for.

"I've decided it's time to get rid of all the poison in my life—starting with you," she stated flatly. "So now that you've relieved your conscience as to the state of my sobriety, why don't you just run on back to your life and finish your masterpiece without any more *inspiration* from your trailer-trash muse?"

Dave struggled to keep his voice level. "I know you're hurt. And I want you to know how proud I am of you for resisting temptation, but you're walking a thin line here so be careful not to say anything today that can't be taken back tomorrow."

That said, he risked life and limb by taking another step toward her. One more and he'd be right on top of her. Kayanne jumped up off the bed to face him toe-to-toe.

"Why shouldn't I? You have no compunction in how you use your words. You can change anything I say with a few lousy keystrokes. You can twist my words to fit your purpose or put your own words in my mouth for that matter. I can't believe you have the gall to tell *me* to be careful what *I* say. How about you being careful what you put down on the page for posterity? For everybody and his dog to read."

"I didn't mean to hurt you," he told her.

Even if that was true, Kayanne wasn't sure that was reason enough to forgive him.

"Maybe not," she said. "But the bottom line is that you weren't even as honest with me as the paparazzi scum who sell their garbage to the tabloids. Even they have more integrity than to literally screw somebody before doing the same to them in print. As far as I'm concerned you can go right on living the rest of your life vicariously through me if that's what you really want to do. But don't ever make the mistake of thinking you can control me off the page."

Kayanne took some satisfaction in seeing his eyes cloud with pain as her words hit their mark. He was lucky. If she'd been a man, she likely would have backed up those words with her fists.

Dave shook his head adamantly. "Sweetheart, I don't want to control you. I just want to be with you."

Kayanne hated herself for secretly thrilling to the endearment he tossed her way. Dave looked so convincingly sorry that she was almost tempted to buy the cheap remorse he was peddling. Almost.

When he reached for her hand, she drew back as if to slap him. To his credit, he didn't so much as flinch.

"Go ahead," he told her. "Hit me if it'll make you feel better. Looking at it from your perspective, I suppose I deserve it."

"You suppose so?"

Kayanne despised the pettiness that marked her tone. As tempting as it might be to leave a red mark across his handsome face, she didn't want to give him the satisfaction—especially since it would just lead to a wrestling match in her bedroom. Not a good idea given the fact that anger and passion were so closely linked. She didn't dare risk the objectivity needed to maintain her present level of fury. Nor could she afford to squander her remaining shred of dignity on one last roll in the hay—one that might very well deposit her back into the bottle and put a cork in it for good.

"I'd like you to read the rest of the book. It's almost finished," Dave said, tentatively broaching the subject. "Spice isn't at all what she seemed to be in the first few chapters, the ones that you read. In fact, I'm hoping that you and the rest of the world will fall in love with her— just like I did."

Kayanne's heart did a slow flip inside her chest. Was he actually admitting that he loved her? Or simply referring to the woman of his imagination, the one he'd christened Spice as a play on her own name? How could she trust anything this man said? He could simply be trying to pacify her so that she didn't sue him to stop publication of his book.

Did he really believe he could make things better just by writing a new ending to his story? Dave may not be vain about his good looks or his privileged background, but Kayanne had never met a writer worth his salt who didn't lay his ego on the line with every word he wrote. Striking out in anger, she landed a hit below the literary belt.

"Better yet, why don't you just kill off Spice, resurrect the impeccable Jasmine, and put her back in your bed where she belongs? You obviously prefer making love to a fantasy over a real woman who is less than perfect. One who actually might have had an interesting life before meeting you."

All the air left Dave's lungs in a single whoosh.

"And while we're on the subject of Jasmine," Kayanne continued, not heeding his advice about watching what came out of her mouth in a fit of rage. "I'm glad I killed her. She was a simpering fool. And as fake as half the boobs on a Los Angeles beach. As far as I'm concerned, she deserved to die, along with all the rest of the one-dimensional characters that men dream up to flatter their big old egos."

Kayanne was surprised to see a tiny smile toy with the edges of Dave's lips.

"You're right," he admitted. "About everything. Right about me using you to advance my story. Right about Jasmine. And most of all, right about me living vicariously through you. The question now is whether or not you'll ever be able to forgive me."

Like a light switch being flipped off, all the fight went out of Kayanne. She understood that part of her struggle with substance abuse was a driving need to be right. Suddenly, being right didn't seem nearly as important as being happy. Especially since that long-term rancor was only going to lead her straight back to the bottle.

Kayanne dropped onto the bed in a posture of defeat. She sat on the edge holding her head in her hands, trying to come to terms with the person she wanted to be. That most definitely wasn't the world-weary cynic that Dave described in his book. There was no white light involved in this acceptance—just an understanding that she, of all people, was obligated to grant forgiveness when it was asked of her.

Especially when she so deeply loved the person asking.

"Don't worry," she said, looking deeply into his eyes and trying to memorize the golden flakes floating in those dark irises. "I won't do anything to stand in the way of getting your book published. Whether or not I took exception to what I read, it was good. Really good. A great improvement over your first book."

Dropping to one knee, Dave did his best to assure her. "The book's insignificant. I'll destroy it if that's what you want. Your feelings are what matter the most to me."

Kayanne shook her head. That wasn't what she wanted. The words he'd written were already burned into her memory never to be erased. Emotionally spent, she saw no reason to punish Dave beyond the hateful things she'd already said to him. She managed a wobbly smile.

"I think you've got a bestseller on your hands. One that should guarantee you'll never have to go home to run the family business unless you decide that you want to. For what it's worth, I really do wish you well."

The furrows in Dave's forehead deepened as he took both of Kayanne's hands in his. "It sounds like you're giving me the brush-off."

"I'm letting you go as a friend."

Dave looked shocked when the enormity of that statement hit him. "You can't possibly mean that we're through."

Kayanne's smile slipped. "It's for the best."

"I'm on my knees," Dave pointed out. "Begging you to give me another chance."

She studied the face that she loved: eyes the color of aged wood, dusty hair soft to the touch, a mouth that smiled generously and often, and tanned skin pulled over angular handsome features. The thought of this man loving anyone else killed her. And yet, she couldn't deny him the opportunity to move on with his life. He had every right to take some fresh-faced coed to the family plantation. Someone his parents would welcome into their family with open arms. Someone like Jasmine.

A note of desperation stole into his voice. "Since I'm down here on my knees already, why don't I go ahead and make it official by proposing?"

It was the last thing Kayanne expected. She didn't know how to react. She didn't even know how much she'd wanted to hear those words until they were actually spoken aloud. All the glamour and glitz of modeling faded into nothingness compared to a lifetime spent with the man she loved. Sharing not only his bed but also his dreams. It was more than she'd ever allowed herself to hope for. Certainly more than anything waiting for her in the big city.

Unfortunately, Dave's proposal felt like an afterthought, something intended to make things right by temporarily smoothing hurt feelings. Not something on which to base a lifetime decision. Kayanne brushed her lips lightly against his. Determined to remain strong, she fought the sob struggling to rise to the surface.

"You shouldn't propose to me because it just wouldn't work."

Her voice was gentled by a truth too painful to be spoken above a whisper.

"Because whatever Spice becomes by the end of your book, *I* can never become anything other than me. Reading those first few chapters made me realize that on some level you'll always be ashamed of me."

Dave hotly protested the ridiculousness of that assertion, but she put a finger to his lips and asked him to let her finish.

"Given our differences in background, education and experiences, your family would never accept a wild child like me. And I can't say that I blame them. My life hasn't exactly been low-profile."

The stricken expression on Dave's face told Kayanne that he'd given this some thought himself before reaching a similar conclusion. While he might conveniently forget to mention to his parents that he was living with her, marriage required family knowledge, involvement and, ultimately, approval. Kayanne didn't want to put that kind of burden on him when it was obvious that he was struggling to separate his needs from theirs as it was.

"It's okay," she assured him, doing her best to sound cavalier. "Can you imagine me at some stuffy academic banquet making small talk with fellow professors about the Shakespearean authorship debate? And their reaction when they discover the only degree I have is a high-school diploma?"

"Who gives a damn about what anybody else thinks?" Dave yelled.

"Believe it or not, I do."

No matter how far she'd come, Kayanne could never outrun her past. Beneath all those slick magazine spreads was a little girl who wouldn't ask friends over to play for fear they would make fun of where she lived.

"Knowing you're ashamed of me would be worse than not having you at all. You have my blessing to end your book however you want, but I'm going to put an end to this real-life relationship right now. I've made up my mind. As soon as I'm sure Mom can get along all right without me, I'll be leaving for New York."

Thirteen

Dave had no doubt Suzanne Aldarmann would manage just fine without her daughter. *He* was the one who couldn't imagine life without Kayanne. Glancing at the nearly finished manuscript that he'd deposited on the kitchen table when he'd first arrived, he cursed it under his breath as he closed the front door of the trailer behind himself.

What a mess he'd made of things.

An eternal optimist, he still held out hope that Kayanne would relent and read the remainder of his book; the best-case scenario being that she would see how Spice's amazing transformation over the course of the novel mirrored his perception of her. And see how much he loved her through prose that truly elevated this book to another level.

She would be moved to give him another chance.

Aside from hoping that this book held the key to repairing their relationship, Kayanne's opinion mattered to him. More than she knew. Though she had a tendency to put herself down for her lack of formal education, Dave valued her judgment as much if not more than the opinions of his colleagues. For one thing, she was brutally honest. And intuitive. Despite popular opinion, one didn't reach the top of the fashion industry by being a bubble head. The few times he'd asked her for help either in plotting or with something more personal, her insight had proven invaluable. It hurt him deeply to hear her refer to herself as his "trailer-park muse."

Of course, Dave knew he could sugarcoat the truth all he wanted, but it wouldn't change the fact that he had used her. Shamelessly.

Never mind that it had been innocent at the start. Writers draw their inspiration from any number of incidents and people who spark their imagination. Life in all its complexities is fair game to them. The point where Dave had crossed the line was in failing to talk to Kayanne about the liberties he'd taken with her life when she'd moved from being a fictional character to his lover.

Furthermore, while it was true that he hadn't portrayed her in the most flattering light after their first contentious meeting, from that moment on she had taken over his life as well as his book. And both were better for it. She breathed fresh air into prose and a life too

laden with concerns about what other people thought—
Dave's parents included.

It would be a lie to say that he hadn't considered the
possibility that they might look down their noses at
Kayanne. Then again, he may have misjudged them—
just as he had her. For all the emphasis they placed on
status, John and Eula Evans's marriage was based on
mutual respect. It was a respect they'd extended to their
only son as well. As much as they hated seeing him
"waste" his talents frittering away his expensive education only to move as far away as he could from the
family business, they ultimately supported his decision
to become whatever he wanted to be. In addition, they
offered him a safety net. One that he'd been less than
gracious in accepting.

The more Dave thought about it, the more he wondered if Kayanne might not fit into his family better than
he himself did. She certainly knew how to appreciate
what was missing in her own life: the stability of a two-
parent family and a love that wasn't based on lies. It was
the kind of life he wanted.

And the kind of life Kayanne deserved.

Dave saw the fact that she'd turned down his proposal
of marriage as simply another obstacle to overcome, not
a reason to give up hope altogether. Time had amazing
healing properties and he prided himself on being a
patient man. He went home to wait for Kayanne to read
the chapters that he'd left for her and fall in love with
them. And with him all over again.

All that was missing was the last couple of chapters.

And a ring.

A great, big, beautiful diamond that proclaimed to the whole world that this amazing woman was his till the end of time. Wanting to shout the news from the rooftops, Dave started by placing a very important, belated long-distance call.

"Mom," he said when she picked up the receiver, "I've met someone…."

A day passed. Then another. Time moved as slowly as brackish water. When Kayanne failed to contact him after the third day, Dave began to worry. She wouldn't take his phone calls. She returned unopened the letter over which he'd agonized. And one morning, he found his manuscript on his doorstep with no indication that she'd read a single word of it.

As his deadline loomed, Dave threw himself into his work, hoping to use his angst as the necessary fuel to finish his book. He prayed that Kayanne would recognize her own wild perfection in the character that she'd spawned. She occupied his every thought and rendered him completely unable to function in any capacity. She was his obsession. Without her in his bed, he couldn't sleep. He couldn't eat. And he damned sure couldn't write.

How much easier it was to write about love from a safe distance than feel it burn in his veins like a lethal injection. He could no more finish his book than he could plug the hole in his chest where his heart used to be. Loneliness filled every nook, cranny and corner of his life. Work lost all meaning for him.

As did life.

Not the type ever to consider suicide, Dave came to a better understanding of how a young boy like Pete Nargas could become so desperate as to actually pull the trigger on himself. Dave developed empathy for every lovesick, besotted character that he'd ever minimized before. In short, he joined the brotherhood of the brokenhearted and was forced to reevaluate his view of the frail human race.

So it was that Rose found him sitting unshaven on his front porch considering a bottle of Jack Daniel's whiskey at ten o'clock one morning. He could hear her tsk-tsking all the way up the sidewalk. And he didn't score any gentleman points by jumping up to help her to her seat, either. She looked around in displeasure at his once-tidy workplace.

"You're looking well," he said, clearing off a place for her.

She really did. There was something different about her. She looked less dowdy. Younger. A paisley silk scarf held artfully with a dragonfly brooch accentuated a new spring-green jacket. And she had artfully applied makeup to a face that wore a more determined look than Dave had ever seen before.

"Wish I could say the same for you," Rose told him, not bothering with social pleasantries. "You're a mess."

She shook her head in disgust and sniffed as if smelling something particularly distasteful. Like a rat foraging in its own filth.

"Nice to see you again, too."

The sarcasm was lost on her. "No wonder Kayanne left you. I would've, too," Rose pointed out, making it apparent that she wasn't in the market for a drunken boyfriend. Clearly she had all her wits about her today.

Being rejected by an octogenarian didn't improve Dave's mood any. He responded in an equally candid manner. "If you don't have anything constructive to say, I'd appreciate you letting me drink in peace."

"Fine. If you don't want to know how Kayanne's doing, I'll just be on my way then," Rose snapped, struggling to get to her feet.

Dave's pulse quickened at the sound of that lyrical name. Hope was resurrected in the rapid beating of his heart. Had she sent a message for him? Anything at all was better than the silence that presently held him imprisoned. He jumped to his feet and did his best to appease the old lady.

"Just sit tight," he told her, "I'll go get the gingersnaps."

He'd deal later with the fact that the only cookies in his pantry were as hard as hockey pucks. Right now, he had to do whatever it took to keep Rose placated until he gleaned every sliver of information about Kayanne that he could. Rose harrumphed, settled into her chair and smoothed out the wrinkles in her skirt.

"Don't bother," she said. "I'm here for one thing, and it's not your lousy cookies. It's to get two people who I care very much about to admit to being fools. After fifty years of marriage to the same man, God rest his soul, I believe I'm qualified to offer a little unsolicited advice in matters of the heart."

Dave leaned forward anxiously. "I'll take any advice you have to offer, Rose."

She nodded sagely. "The truth is I can't stand seeing either one of you two kids let pride stand in the way of your happiness. Trust me. True love is a gift that isn't offered often in this life so you'd better hold tight to it when it comes around."

Having been duly chastised, Dave proceeded to shoot a barrage of questions at her.

"How is she? Has she said anything about me? Did she read anything I sent over? Has she changed her mind about leaving?"

Shaking her head, Rose clucked in disapproval. "The poor thing's terrible. Ever since she quit, all she does is mope around. Nobody wants to see her go back to New York. That girl's the best thing to happen to the Manor since they opened their doors. She's organized socials, gotten the ladies feeling pretty again, and done more for the old fellas' libidos than Viagra. She's even got a beau lined up for me. A nice fellow by the name of Joe Hansen."

Blushing, she stopped to shake a bony finger at Dave. "Then you had to go and ruin everything by breaking her heart."

A selfish part of him was glad to hear that Kayanne was having trouble functioning without him. That meant she still had feelings for him. Such encouraging news was overshadowed by the prospect of her leaving. For good.

"I proposed to her," he said in his defense.

It wasn't easy admitting that she'd flatly turned him down, but Dave didn't much appreciate the entire senior citizenry holding him solely responsible for depriving them of their one bright spot of the day, either.

"How?" Rose asked bluntly. "Did you have a big, old expensive ring in a black velvet box with you at the time? Did you plan out what you were going to say and pop the question in some romantic place and in some heart-felt way? Or did you just sort of casually mention that since you were already down on your knees begging for-giveness for being a jackass that you might as well pro-pose in some offhanded way that any proud woman might interpret as an afterthought? Or worse yet as a way to ease your own conscience about hurting her so badly?"

Adrift in his own pain, Dave hadn't ever looked at it like that. The fact that Rose knew the details of his failed proposal told him that she was in Kayanne's con-fidence. While that bothered him on some level, it also held out a glimmer of hope.

"At least I've got her to stop talking about leaving until after the fashion show," Rose continued. "That means you've got until the end of the month to pull your head out of your heinie and set things right. Make her see how much you really love her. And need her. And want her."

Visions of caveman techniques came to mind, but as Rose had already pointed out, a gentle touch was called for. Kayanne had been muscled by too many men in her life already, and none of them had been able to force her to do anything she didn't want to.

"Fashion show?"

Rose opened her purse and drew out an invitation, which she handed him.

"I'm counting on you to be there," she said before stiffly getting to her feet and leaving him to figure the rest out for himself.

There was a commotion in the dressing room that demanded Kayanne's immediate attention. She was all too familiar with the nerves, squabbling and power struggles that went with putting on a fashion show. But the smiles, laughter and camaraderie that met her as she stepped into the crowded room was something altogether new. All around her, stunning women were having the time of their lives.

The fact that they were senior citizens didn't lessen the satisfaction Kayanne felt as she surveyed their glowing faces. If Rose had taught her anything, it was that a woman was entitled to feel beautiful all the days of her life. The seed for this fashion extravaganza had been planted the first time Kayanne had accompanied Rose to a boutique and had found nothing appropriate in stock. It had occurred to her then that this was an age group the industry had all but forgotten. In a business that generated over a hundred and seventy billion dollars a year, it was virtually an untapped market.

Her mistake had been in mentioning it to Rose, who had been pushing her ever since to undertake a new venture. Rose had promised to act as a silent partner and put up the capital to launch a new line designed especially for older women. Kayanne's mother had wanted in as well. It seemed she hadn't squandered all the money her daughter had sent her on missionaries and con men after all. She had a healthy portion stashed safely away making steady if not spectacular interest. Added to the local support were big-name backers who'd already expressed an interest in marketing Kayanne's name and designs.

"When have you ever been able to remain silent on anything?" Kayanne had asked Rose, a fact underscored when the older lady had wheedled from her the details of her break-up with Dave. Rose could no more remain quiet on that issue than on matters of politics or religion. Ever since meeting Joe Hansen, she had been feeling particularly generous and wanted everyone to share in the joy of her budding romance. She seemed to feel personally obligated to set things right between Kayanne and Dave.

"You deserve to be happy," Rose had told her.

"What we deserve and what we get are often two different things," had been Kayanne's wry reply.

Nonetheless, the idea of marketing her own brand of specialty clothing was intriguing. As was Rose's suggestion that they hold a fashion show to launch the idea and get a grassroots feel for whether it was truly worth pursuing. There was something appealing about designing clothes for women who could never grow too old for the runway. Something about designing for women who'd seen enough of the world to value comfort and style equally. The only thing keeping Kayanne in town right now was her mother's health, which was improving every day, and the fashion show that Rose had inveigled her into putting on.

They'd arranged to use the community hall for the evening, and Kayanne was astonished to see a packed house when she peeked out from behind the curtain. People of all ages crowded in to see their grandmothers, mothers, wives and sweethearts strut their stuff. If tonight's reception was any indication, she might actually have a chance of selling her new line of clothing when she got back to Manhattan, a place whose glitter had lost much of its shine for her.

Suddenly Kayanne found herself desperately missing Dave. She wished he was there to share this moment with her. To hold her hand and settle her nerves with his steady humor—and his mind-blowing kisses. Her throat tightened around the object stuck there. It could well have been her heart. She cursed Dave soundly for intruding on her thoughts at the most inopportune times. Like every other minute of the day. That only made it all the more difficult to focus on the crisis at hand.

"What's the problem?"

Kayanne assumed a light tone with the assembled crowd in the dressing room. She was afraid some of the ladies might be getting cold feet and didn't want to have to confiscate any alcohol being used to steady anyone's nerves. The way she was feeling at the moment, Kayanne wasn't sure she'd be strong enough to resist taking a swig herself.

"Why did you call me in here anyway? It looks to me like everything's under control."

Rose stepped forward to a round of polite applause and presented Kayanne with a huge bouquet of fresh flowers.

"Whatever happens out there tonight, we just want to thank you for what you've done for us. For making us feel desirable again."

Kayanne looked around the room and saw nothing but smiling, grateful faces. All of the women gathered about were gray and wrinkled. Some were still grieving missing breasts from mastectomies and until now hadn't ever been able to find clothes that didn't make them feel freakishly self-conscious. A few would need walkers to help them down the makeshift runway. Swathed in a rainbow's array of colors and textures, they were all incredibly beautiful.

And brave.

"I'm so proud of you," Kayanne said, giving each one a flower from the bouquet to carry during her debut. More nervous for her elderly friends than she'd ever been for herself, she checked her watch and announced, "It's almost time to get this show on the road."

Five minutes later, she was sitting in the front row directly in front of the runway watching the curtain go up. Butterflies danced in her stomach and doubts toyed with her mind.

What if one of the models falls and breaks a hip?

What if the audience doesn't like my designs?

What if they laugh?

Or boo?

Who in the world do I think I am trying to launch a new line in Podunk, Wyoming, when there are over five thousand designer showrooms in New York alone?

Sitting next to her, Kayanne's mother squeezed her

hand and gave her a reassuring smile. "Everything's going to be just fine."

It seemed only fitting that Rose was the first model of the evening. She shimmered down the runway in a mid-length dress of pale blue that was appropriate for attending a formal affair or simply dining out at an elegant restaurant. With all the aplomb of a seasoned veteran, she smiled at Kayanne, blew a kiss to Joe Hansen who was sitting behind her, and tossed a lily over her shoulder to a young lady sitting with her grandfather. The audience was utterly enchanted.

Kayanne heaved a sigh of relief and settled in her seat to enjoy the rest of a very special evening. She didn't know exactly how special it was going to prove to be until Rose stepped out from behind the curtain after the last model had completed her turn.

"As a finale to tonight's festivities, we have a special guest who is going to model his own version of humble pie for us," she announced with a sly wink.

Then she reached through the curtain and exchanged places with Dave in a move that proved she could have been a magician's assistant as well as a fashion model. Kayanne's palms grew sweaty at the sight of the man she loved dressed in a white tuxedo with tails, holding a dozen red roses and looking better than any airbrushed model she'd ever seen. He looked terribly nervous. That this clearly was beyond his comfort level only endeared him to Kayanne all the more. She couldn't imagine what Rose had done to get him to agree to such a public exhibition, but the instant that he stepped out onto that stage, she knew she didn't want to live another minute without him.

He cleared his throat, stared into the lights, and deliberately sought her out. He began his long journey down the runway to the hoots and hollers of an audience delighted to be getting far more than they had paid for. Dave stopped at the end of the runway and looked directly at Kayanne. Bending down on one knee, he cleared his throat.

"It was brought to my attention that my earlier proposal lacked a certain romantic appeal. This is my clumsy attempt to remedy that. I want everybody in this room and the entire world to know how much I love you, Kayanne. If I promise to never, ever hurt you again, would you please consider making me the happiest man alive by agreeing to be my wife?"

As moved by the trickle of sweat running down the side of his face as by the elegantly wrapped box that he pulled out of his jacket pocket, Kayanne knew how hard it was for him to so publicly put himself on the line. Any nagging doubts that he might have proposed before only to assuage her hurt feelings dissolved, along with her fear that he was secretly ashamed of her. A man didn't risk this level of embarrassment unless he felt anything other than the most convincing love.

Rose was right. She was a fool.

Kayanne stood on wobbly legs to take the roses from him.

"Say yes!" called out one overly involved onlooker, setting off a chain of such cheers.

"Go on, honey," her mother urged, dabbing her eyes with a tissue.

Dave helped her up onto the runway by way of a strategically placed stepladder. Juggling his flowers, she accepted a ring box from him and held it up so that the audience could take a peek.

"It's perfect," she said over their oohs and aahs.

Then she wrapped her arms around his neck and kissed him fully on the lips. Any resistance to the idea of spending the rest of her life with this man melted beneath the heat of a flame destined to burn throughout eternity.

The crowd roared.

"Yes!" Kayanne told him through a blur of tears. "Yes, I'll marry you."

Dave refused to let go of her. His arms remained anchored solidly around her waist as he whispered in her ear. "I'll burn the manuscript if you want me to."

"Over my dead body," she whispered back. "I love what you've done with my character. And more importantly what you've done to me. To us."

Dave's eyes lit up with the realization that she'd actually read the chapters he'd given her. And liked them. With Kayanne by his side, he couldn't imagine anything keeping him from achieving all of his dreams. He beamed.

"Just be careful not to make Spice too good in the final chapters," she warned, fearing his tendency to swing from one extreme to the other. "And remember. You're marrying a real woman, mister. One with real emotions, a checkered past and immediate needs...."

Only more than happy to oblige on that last count,

Dave was forced to settle for what was audience appropriate at the moment, promising to meet those needs more completely once he got her where he wanted her in his bed. Bending her deeply at the back, he gave the crowd the finale they wanted—a real old-fashioned Hollywood kiss.

Basking in the thunderous applause as a cast of sexy senior citizens joined them on stage, Kayanne felt she'd finally come home. Home to a man who loved her for who she was. A man who understood that love alone had the power to change a beast into a beauty—from the inside out. Home to a life that made her feel productive and happy. Home to the belief that she deserved a happy ending just the same as any character her husband chose to put in his next bestseller.

Real life just didn't get any better than that.

Silhouette® Desire®

What Happens in Vegas…

Their Million-Dollar Night

by

KATHERINE GARBERA

(SD #1720)

Roxy O'Malley is just the kind of hostess
corporate sophisticate Max Williams needs
for some R & R while at the casinos. Will one
white-hot night lead to a trip to the altar?

**Don't miss the exciting conclusion
to WHAT HAPPENS IN VEGAS…
available this April from
Silhouette Desire.**

On Sale April 2006
Available at your favorite retail outlet.

If you enjoyed what you just read,
then we've got an offer you can't resist!

Take 2 bestselling
love stories FREE!
Plus get a FREE surprise gift!

THE ELLIOTTS

Mixing Business with Pleasure

The saga continues with

The Forbidden Twin

by

SUSAN CROSBY

(SD #1717)

Scarlet Elliott's secret crush is finally unveiled
as she takes the plunge and seduces her twin
sister's ex-fiancé. The relationship is forbidden,
the attraction…undeniable.

On Sale April 2006

*Available at your
favorite retail outlet.*

COMING NEXT MONTH

SDCNM0306